IN FLAMES

PHOENIX: LEXTAL CHRONICLES #2

ELISE FABER

IN FLAMES
by Elise Faber

Newsletter sign-up

IN FLAMES
Copyright © 2021 ELISE FABER
Print ISBN: 978-1-946140-98-2
eBook ISBN: 978-1-946140-97-5
Cover Art by Jena Brignola

FIRE

FLAMES. Ash. Heat and cinder.

Tearing through and destroying everything in its path, and even after it's extinguished, its embers can be fanned to life, causing massive amounts of destruction in no time at all. Lush greenery can become blackened fields, felled forests, acre after acre of dark, *empty* space.

But eventually, that black transforms into green, the soil growing richer, the fields more fertile. Trees sprout and slowly begin their ascent into the sky.

Slowly, the emptiness becomes full.

Of life.

Of love.

ONE

Suz

ANOTHER DATE.

Another loser.

Sighing, she waited long enough so the man—said loser—would have vacated the hallway, then she slipped out of her room and made her way to the infirmary.

It was empty, but she could always find something to keep her busy.

And, if she waited long enough, someone would get hurt and she'd have something real to do, something that wasn't sitting around reviewing charts and being jealous because her friends were ridiculously happy and bonded and . . . she was dating losers.

Which wasn't *entirely* fair.

The Rengalla she'd gone out with that evening was a perfectly nice man.

Just not the one for her.

And, if she were being completely honest, he was a little boring.

As her life had been . . . for decades.

Nearly a hundred years old, she'd lived through medical and technological advancements, she'd lived through wars and loss, and . . . she was bored out of her mind.

She wanted excitement.

She wanted to feel something, *anything* aside from this heavy weight sitting on her chest.

The one that told her she was missing out, missing *something*.

Not doing enough. Not helping enough. Not living—

Enough.

Yes, that was a trend with her.

Well, that and lonely.

Unfortunately, lonely was also a trend. Because as much as the men she'd dated had waxed poetic about liking strong women, that hadn't actually come to fruition, especially when she was pulled out of dinner or bed or sexy, fun naked time and called into the infirmary because someone had broken their leg, or burned their arm, or because a baby had decided to make an untimely arrival.

Then they realized that dating the Rengalla's top healer wasn't all fun and games.

Then they tolerated the intrusion a time or five, maybe even ten.

But eventually they tired of the interruptions, of not being first in her priorities and then . . . they went away.

So circling back to lonely. And she might as well add horny into that mix.

Because that was the crux of it, too. She was tired of her hand and her vibrator. She wanted an orgasm courtesy of someone else. She wanted someone to look at her with desire. To want her. No, to *need* her.

Like Dee had Cody.

Like Gabby had Mason.

Like she would probably *never* have.

Sighing, she grabbed the doorknob, started to push into the infirmary. Maybe she wouldn't ever bond or have a man devoted to her like her friends did, "But, is it too much for me to have just *one* night of hot sex?"

"Pent up, Suzie girl?"

That voice.

Liquid honey down her spine, heat drifting between her thighs, desire making the tips of her fingers itch—

To release her magic, to wipe that smirk off his gorgeous face.

To . . . wrap her fingers in the strands of his deep brown hair and yank his head down for a kiss.

She let go of the knob and turned to face Graham.

Cocky, funny Graham.

Whom *everyone* liked. Who was nice to every Rengalla, big and small.

Every Rengalla, except for her.

Her he liked to torment.

She couldn't stand the man—or at least that was what she told herself. Plus, he was too arrogant by half and never failed to infuriate her. But he wasn't dating anyone, and clearly after this evening, she wasn't either.

And . . . she wanted him, had spent *years* wanting him while pretending not to.

She stepped toward him, close enough to smell his scent—all damp forest floor and warm summer sunshine—close enough to feel the heat from his body, sense his strength in the hard planes of his body.

"You offering to help me out?" she asked, taking another step, her breasts brushing against his chest.

A muscle ticked in his jaw. "Suz," he muttered, moving back and putting some distance between them. "Don't be ridiculous."

Hurt.

God, it sliced right through her, tore at her insides.

Not even the man who'd slept with half the single women in the Colony wanted her.

Cool.

She forced a laugh, her eyes burning. So stupid. "Right," she said and spun around, reached for the knob once again. "I'm busy. Now, go away."

"Wait." He grabbed her arm.

She shook him off, pushed into the space that had become her sanctuary. Maybe there were some bandages to organize, some charts to file—

Click.

That wasn't the sound of the door closing.

Rather, it was the sound of the door *locking*.

On a gasp, she spun around.

Graham was there, eyes hot as he stepped away from the door. "So, little Suzie girl is feeling needy," he said, the words sending a shiver down her spine. He crowded into her. "She wants my help scratching that itch—"

She lifted her chin. "Go to he—"

He kissed her.

TWO

Graham

HE SHOULDN'T BE HERE.

And he really fucking shouldn't be doing this.

This being his mouth pressed to Suz's lush lips, his hands on her hips, pulling her flush against him.

She was a *baby*.

She was friends with his younger sister, for God's sake.

He was one hundred and twelve years older than her, and while their long lifespans meant that the Rengalla didn't often worry about age gaps, a century more of experience was . . . well, an entire lifetime.

Plus, she was friends with his sister.

Who was young and innocent and . . . *young*.

Suz was *too* young.

For him to have his hands on her. His lips pressed to hers. His tongue inside her mouth.

Shame whipped through him, slicing his insides to ribbons, and he dropped his hands, started to lift his head.

Then she moaned.

A soft, rasping noise that emerged from her throat, vibrated against his lips, licked down his skin like flames. And instead of letting her go, instead of moving to the door and getting back on with his day, he wrapped his arms tighter around her and . . . kissed her like his magic was fading and this was his last day on Earth.

And she responded.

Oh, how she responded—melting against him, her lush breasts flush against his chest, her fingers wrapping tight in his hair, her tongue dancing against his as she kissed him back until his head spun. Her hands slipped under the hem of his T-shirt, trailed across his abdomen, dipped under the waistband of his jeans.

Fuck, that was good.

Fuck, that was *really* good.

Fuck, that was good enough to make him forget all about the age difference and to let his fingers do some slipping and sliding of their own.

He released her lips to allow them both to suck in some much-needed air then began kissing his way along her jaw, down her throat.

Citrus and cloves, tart and spice. The scent that was so intrinsically Suz filled his senses. That perfume was imprinted into her skin, floated like a cloud around her hair, made him feel like she was surrounding every inch of him. And being this close to her, closer than he'd ever allowed himself before—or realistically, he hadn't allowed himself to be this close since the moment his body had recognized hers as an adult—was both the greatest pleasure and absolute torture.

She was a woman.

A woman he wanted.

When she'd gone away to college, she'd still been a girl,

bright and innocent and all lanky limbs and freckle-covered nose. She'd gotten her degree then had gone to medical school, completed her residency, when it was safer, when their enemy hadn't been so good at hunting them.

God, he could still remember the day she'd left. He'd been on a normal patrol, had watched her from the trees surrounding the Colony, entranced by the way she'd hugged her family and friends goodbye, so much care in each of the embraces. She'd waved off help as she'd loaded a couple of suit-cases in the back of her VW Bug, her hair long and straight, tie-dye and bell-bottoms covering her lanky frame. Then with a wave, she'd gotten in the car and driven off, excitement on her face.

She'd left a sweet, youthful girl looking forward to the future.

Then she'd come back, almost a decade later, a woman—the real world written on the lines of her face, the shadows in her eyes. Maturity that comes from experience and yet still that wealth of compassion beneath.

He'd arrested, completely frozen in place when he'd first laid eyes on her upon her return.

He could remember that moment with crystal clarity, too.

An arm around his sister's waist, curves filling out tight jeans, breasts pushing out the cotton of her T-shirt. Simple clothes, and yet, the sexiest outfit he'd ever laid eyes on. Every instinct in his body had screamed at him to close the distance between them, to stake a claim right then and there.

She wasn't so innocent.

But . . . she was still young. Still his sister's friend.

And still too many years, too many experiences between them. She needed someone her age, someone without his baggage.

But when her eyes had met his, wide and warm, her lips

curved into a tempting smile, he'd nearly forgotten about all of his reasons to stay away.

Which was the moment he'd realized he needed to withdraw.

A tactical retreat in order to keep his distance.

Except . . . he wasn't keeping his distance tonight. He was really fucking close, and it was absolutely glorious.

Suz wasn't wearing her usual T-shirt and jeans—she'd kept the latter but swapped out the former for a shining piece of black silk that clung to her curves and made him want to trace his fingers over the glittering material . . . then beneath it.

"Come here," she whispered, gripping the sides of his face, tugging his head up from her throat, and taking his mouth in a kiss that showed exactly how much she'd grown up. Confident and demanding, he'd never had anything hotter than this woman pressed up against him, kissing him until his lungs screamed for oxygen.

Eventually though, they needed to breathe, so he released her lips, trailing his mouth along her jaw, reveling in the soft moans, the way her fingers grew tighter in his hair.

But he couldn't kiss the parts he wanted to reach.

She was short, and he was tall, and he couldn't become a fucking pretzel, much as he was trying.

Luckily, he was also strong.

A senior soldier, he was trained to protect his people—and that didn't mean just using his magic. He was deadly in hand-to-hand combat, a decent marksman, and prided himself on being a tough motherfucker.

His mother had told him more than once as a child that it was okay to cry if he was hurting, that he was allowed to be sad after his father had died.

But Graham wasn't like that.

Tie it down, buckle it tight, be a *man*, and make sure she was okay, his sister was okay.

Make sure they *all* were okay. He'd do it, serve his people, care for those who were vulnerable until his last breath.

Just like his father.

Except . . . he wasn't really thinking about his father, his past, his centuries on this planet. Or not for long, anyway.

Because Suz was in his arms, those glorious breasts pressed to his chest, her scent surrounding him, her hands dragging his head back up as she slanted her lips across his. Her tongue in his mouth, fingers sliding from his hair to grip his shoulders. He shifted, slipping his hands under her thighs and lifting her up into his arms, coaxing her to straddle his hips, and holding back a moan when she pressed against the hard jut of his erection.

And still, he kissed her. Or maybe she was kissing him.

Either way, any concerns about the past, their differences disappeared. She rocked against his cock, sending desire flooding through him, making sparks coalesce in the corners of his vision. And just that—her in his arms, riding him—was the hottest fucking sexual experience of his life, and they were both still fully clothed.

Speaking of which. He wanted to get them some place horizontal. Hell, vertical, diagonal, upside down, he didn't give a fuck.

He just wanted to go somewhere he could get Suz naked.

Immediately.

"Where?" he asked, pulling his mouth free and nipping at the shell of her ear.

"My office," she moaned, fingers digging into his shoulders, thighs tightening around his waist. "Hurry. I—"

He didn't need to be told twice.

He'd had five decades of pretending he didn't notice the luscious curves she was packing, the ass that filled out the backside of her jeans and made a man imagine way too many ways to pay homage to those squeezable globes, the breasts that would overfill his hands, thighs that were strong and capable and felt fucking incredible beneath his palms, even still encased in denim.

Rapid steps brought him down the hall, to the office where he'd seen her working late many a night.

Come to think of it, he'd also seen her here many an early morning.

Which brought to mind the question of when this woman actually slept, and if she was taking care of herself, and—

His mind went blank.

Because the moment he'd crossed the threshold to her office, she wiggled out of his arms and shimmied out of the sleek black top she was wearing.

His mouth went dry.

His cock grew harder.

Lace. Pale lavender that brought out the gold tones in her skin, the dusky pink of her nipples just barely evident through the material of her bra. His eyes trailed down the softness of her abdomen to the jeans . . . well, to the button of her jeans. Because her fingers were there, flicking open the circle of metal.

The noise as she drew down the zipper was loud in the silence of the room.

Then . . . more pale lace.

Her mouth quirked when he managed to drag his gaze back up to hers. "You like?"

He liked. *Way* too fucking much. Except . . . "Why are you wearing it?" he asked, a bolt of annoyance shooting through him.

Or maybe it wasn't annoyance so much as jealousy.

She shouldn't have dressed with care, planning to sleep with someone else, then jump him in the hall.

He should be special and hers—*only* hers.

Dumbass.

Him.

Because she didn't belong to him, and if she wanted to sleep with someone, he didn't have one fucking right to say anything about it. Guilt slid through him at that thought, enough to clear the haze of desire and make him step back a pace.

Suz couldn't be his. She was Amelia's.

Amelia's friend.

Her *young* friend.

A husky chuckle.

"You think my underwear was for *him?*" She shoved down her jeans, stepped out of the black flats and denim then moved toward him in that skimpy lace set of undergarments.

One finger trailed down his chest.

Plump lips curved up.

"Oh, no, honey," she murmured. "I wear it for *me.*"

Fire licking the base of his spine, his cock hardening farther. He slipped his fingers into her pale brown hair, reveling in the silken locks, the way it made her scent assault his senses anew.

Tilting her head back, he pressed his lips to the base of her throat and inhaled deeply.

"You smell incredible," he growled.

Hands on his biceps, clutching tight. "S-so do you," she said then hissed when he nipped lightly at the place where throat met shoulder and dragged his mouth across her collarbone.

And down.

Down.

But hell, she hadn't grown a foot in the last few minutes, so it wasn't long before he was getting a crick in his neck and feeling frustrated that he couldn't reach all the parts he wanted.

Thankfully, he could think on his feet.

He walked her backward, pressed her against her desk. The

top cluttered with papers and office supplies, coffee mugs and pencils. "These files important?"

"Wh-what?" she asked, breathing hard, her hands running up and down his chest, her chocolate brown eyes clouded with desire.

"These papers important?" Graham nodded toward the stacks of files.

"No," she said and grinned.

But before he could ask her why she was smiling, why there was mischief in her eyes, she turned, extended a hand, and shoved everything off the surface of her desk. The contents hit the floor in a flurry of noise—folders and papers, the empty mug and picture frame, pencils and pens, paperclips and Post-Its and rubber bands all colliding with the tile, exploding around them like confetti.

He'd imagined a few papers hitting the ground.

This was . . . chaos.

But before he could focus too fully on the mess, she spun back to face him, a huge grin on her face. "I'm going to hate myself in the morning when I have to clean that up." Hands slipping under his T-shirt, gripping his waist, and tugging him closer even as she sat on the edge of the desk and spread her thighs. "But I've always wanted to do that."

He grinned. "Living on the edge, sweetheart?"

"The office supply edge?" A snort. "Yeah, that's the extent of my wildness." She traced light patterns on his stomach. "I'm boring."

He chuckled.

Somehow, he didn't think the woman who wore lavender lace and toppled desktops and so confidently pulled him close was anything close to boring.

He brushed his thumb over her cheek. "Nice try, but I saw you," he whispered, remembering the last time the Dalshie—the enemy who'd made it their life's work to eradicate their people—had attacked. Suz had fought being evacuated, but in the end, she'd relented, knowing that as their strongest healer, the vulnerable needed her. But she'd come back the moment it was safe, and she'd stayed and healed their people until her body gave out. Then she'd gotten up and done it all again the next day. Maybe she hadn't killed the enemy firsthand, but she'd given herself, life and limb, to protect her people. So, even with the lace and confidence, she was as much of a soldier as he was.

Brows drawing down, her head tilting slightly to the side. "What do you mean?"

He tucked a strand of her hair behind her. "I saw you out there with us, risking your life for our people. Healing until you passed out."

A shrug. "It's my job to heal people."

Such a Suz thing to say.

"Also," she murmured. "I don't want to talk about my work." She wound her arms around his neck. "I want you to go back to kissing me."

"You sure?" he asked, even though his cock felt ready to snap in half. His head had cleared slightly, enough for him to remember why he'd purposefully kept his distance all these years. He didn't want her to have regrets in the morning.

Regrets aside from the office supplies.

Her hands slid down his chest. "I'm sure."

He brushed her hands aside and stripped off his shirt. "Are you sure it's me you want and not your date?"

Fuck.

Why had he asked that, allowed jealousy to creep back in?

This was a woman he'd spent years *not* wanting. Except . . . that had been a lie, a ruse, a way to protect her from the mess he was inside.

Pink tinged her cheeks, but she reached for the button of his jeans, flicked it open, and tugged down his zipper. "Maybe I should ask *you* that question," she muttered, shoving the material down his thighs. "You're the one who seems to have made it your job to avoid me, while simultaneously dating every single female *except* me."

Not *every* female.

But also not her.

And for good reason.

Because he'd known he would end up in this very position— hard and aching and ready to fuck her into oblivion.

"I've always been convinced you don't even like me," she said as he stepped out of his boots. "For all I know, this is sympathy sex or angry, annoyed sex or . . . well, pity sex because poor little Suz is pathetic and lonely and boring—" She stopped, that pink on the tops of her cheekbones turning bright red. "You know what? We shouldn't do this. I—"

He cupped her jaw, turned her gaze back to his. "This isn't pity sex or angry sex or even sympathy sex." A brush of his lips across hers. "I've wanted you since you came back to the Colony after medical school."

Wide eyes on his. "Then why . . ."

That wasn't a question he wanted to answer. He didn't want to keep bringing thoughts of his sister into this moment, to bring in the sense of responsibility he felt to protect those around him, to question the morality of this situation and the moral code he lived by.

To not take advantage of those who needed protecting.

And Suz needed protecting.

Suz *needed* protecting.

Pieces shifted in his mind.

Suz. Needed. Protecting.

She needed someone to make sure she didn't work too late

and too often. She needed someone to remind her to eat, to get some sleep.

She needed . . . him.

She *needed* him.

"It wasn't the right time back then," he murmured, stroking his fingers down her throat, her skin like silk, goose bumps pebbling to life, her body drifting toward his. "So tell me, Firefly, is tonight the right time?"

Brown eyes going wide, her lips parting and tempting him to kiss.

But he had to know.

Did she really want this?

The uncertainty left those chocolate irises, and her hand covered his cheek, tilted his head down until their lips were a hairsbreadth apart. "Tonight is the perfect time."

His magic—coiled and always at the ready—bucked in the back of his mind, threatened to burst free. That slip of control was unusual. He'd mastered his powers years ago, hadn't ever really struggled to keep it under check, once he'd been taught how.

"Yeah?" he asked, pushing that slip away, focusing on the sexy woman in front of him.

She grinned. "Yeah. Because I think I like being wild and living on the edge."

He nipped at her bottom lip. "I thought you said you were boring?"

"I've decided that I'm living on the edge . . . of an orgasm, and you're going help me out." An innocent look, fluttering lashes, the corners of that sexy mouth tipping up.

"That was a terrible joke," he murmured, nuzzling her throat. "Even by your standards."

"Hey! My jokes aren't—"

"Bad?" He bent and sucked her nipple into his mouth,

loving the way she moaned and arched against him. "They're terrible." He peeled the lace back, rolled the tight bud between thumb and forefinger. "But I think I can help you out with the orgasm edge thing you've got going on."

A hand reaching down, stroking him. "You promise?"

He bit back a groan, focused on the task at hand. "I got you, Firefly."

THREE

Suz

I GOT YOU.

Normally, such a sentiment would make her roll her eyes.

Especially from a pretty boy with golden irises and shining brown hair.

But the man had confidence and swagger and—fine—he kissed like a fucking god.

And . . . she wanted him.

So badly and for so long.

Suz knew this was probably a terrible idea, but he was here. He was looking at her like he actually saw her as a woman and not an asexual creature whose only purpose was to patch up broken bones and deliver babies.

Of course, maybe she felt like everyone saw her that way because *she* saw herself that way.

"Second thoughts?" he asked, brushing her hand aside, his rasping voice sliding over her skin, raising goose bumps, making her shiver.

"No."

A chuckle that had her thighs clenching around his waist. "Just no?"

"Yup."

Fingers brushing along her jaw. "Then why the sad?"

Why was he pushing this? They were both nearly naked, and she was wet and aching and . . . she wanted him to be kissing her again, for him to make her forget where she was, her name, her loneliness. But she was Suz. She was the head healer, and that meant she was supposed to be strong and capable and certainly not unfeeling, but at least in control of her emotions at all times. Which is why she lifted her chin and told him, "The only reason I'm sad is because I haven't had an orgasm in way too long, and we're wasting an eternity talking instead of fucking."

His lips curved into a cocky smile.

"What do you know about fucking?" One finger trailing down her chest, so close to her breasts that she was absolutely desperate for him to touch, to cup, to stroke.

And he was asking her what she knew about fucking.

Delaying.

Making her feel like a child when she'd been a grown woman for ages.

Irritation flooded through her. "I know plenty," she snapped. "And maybe I know that I should get dressed and go find someone else."

That smile didn't fade.

That hand slid to the side, cupped her breast, and if she hadn't been sitting on the edge of the desk, her knees would have wobbled and, okay, would have probably given way. "Hmm. I know you won't do that."

"Why wouldn't I?"

Because she knew about sex and fucking and even making sweet love, but she didn't know about *this*.

The draw. The absolute desperation that had pushed its way inside her, gripped her tightly between its canines and was shaking her fiercely. She wanted his cock thrusting home. She wanted to push him away and to run screaming from the room. She wanted completion. She wanted to release her magic, wrap him up in it, and hold him close. She wanted—

Graham.

More in this moment than she ever had before.

"And I know I want you to stop talking." She hissed out a breath when his thumb stroked her nipple through the lace. "And take me." His golden eyes flared with desire. "Or I *will* find someone else."

"Stop talking about another man when I'm about to fuck you." He nipped her throat.

"And yet, more talking," she said cuttingly. "But still, no fucking."

A growl that raised the hairs on her nape. "I'm trying to make sure you want to do this."

"No. You want me pissed off and muddled, so I fight with you," she snapped. "Because you love nothing more than to make me lose my temper."

He froze, irritation leaving his face, that cocky grin making a reappearance. "Maybe."

She made a noise in outrage. His admission wasn't a surprise exactly—she'd known what she said was the truth—but she was still annoyed by the easy way he'd admitted it. "Why do you live to torment me?" she groaned, head tipping back, gaze on the ceiling.

"Because"—hot breath on her skin—"you've tormented me from the day you came back. Because you're tormenting me with golden skin and lavender lace. Because you smell like oranges and spice, and I want to taste every inch of you." A flick of his tongue across a sensitive spot on her neck. "Yes, I like teasing you. Yes, I like pissing you off. But it's mostly because I think you're fucking beautiful when you're furious."

Her chest heaved as though she'd run a marathon—and she despised marathons and running and . . . well, all forms of exercise—but that wasn't why she couldn't form words.

It was because *his* words were . . .

What?

More than she'd expected from the man who seemed to torment and avoid her in equal terms.

Yes. *That.*

But also . . . so much more than she'd ever expected a man to say about *her* in particular. Because, putting aside his aims to piss her off, she didn't inspire pretty speeches about golden skin or her scent.

She was Suz.

Doctor first. Friend second. Daughter third. Woman . . . a dismal forth.

"I never would have allowed myself to do this," he said, dropping demanding lips onto hers, stealing her breath in a kiss that had her pulse thundering and her lungs struggling even more. "But you let me in, Firefly. You gave me a glimpse, and you need me and, fuck, but I've wanted you for so long."

Her magic bucked in the back of her mind, a tightening coil that threatened to burst outward, that urged her to loosen her control and let it flow free.

Perhaps if she hadn't been quite so desperate, she would have recognized the signs.

Perhaps she would have been able to control herself, to grasp on to the niggling in the back of her mind and pull it forward, tease out its meaning.

Perhaps. Perhaps. *Perhaps.*

Because those were all hypotheticals.

Because in that moment, she didn't find control or question the desire she felt.

In that moment, she let go.

Probably because he reached around her and unclasped her bra, sliding the lace down her arms and tossing it to the side. Maybe also because he slid calloused palms around to her front, up her torso, and cupped her breasts.

But mostly because . . .

She wanted him and this might be the only chance she'd get to have him.

Decision made, she snaked a hand down his chest, slipping her fingers beneath the waistband of his boxer briefs and gripping the hard length of him.

"Now, Graham. *Please.*"

He made a sound she didn't know how to describe. Half-animalistic, half-need. All scorching desire—or maybe that was just her.

Her need. *Her* desire.

Her—

She gasped when he bent his head and sucked her nipple into his mouth. No warning. No finesse or gentleness. This was a beast released, a man past his edge, and . . . it was fucking glorious.

He brushed her hands off his cock, and though she missed the hard length of him against her palms, what he did next was even better.

Namely, lifting her off the desk long enough to strip her out of her panties before setting her back down and kneeling between her legs. "Yes?" he asked, pressing a kiss to the inside of one thigh.

"Hell fucking yes."

He smirked, and she realized that she'd said that aloud, but before she could feel any embarrassment—and frankly, if she were being truthful with herself, there wasn't any embarrass-ment. Need, yes. But not shame.

Not with the way Graham was looking at her.

Then there were no more thoughts of emotions or how he was looking at her or regrets or anything that wasn't pleasure.

Because it was a fuck-ton of pleasure.

A *fuck-ton*.

His tongue traced up, dipping into the crease of her thigh, making her shiver. Then . . . he kissed her, gave her the absolute best kiss of her life, and it wasn't on her mouth. He dipped closer, circled her clit and sucked deeply, sliding a finger through the wet heat of her before slipping it inside.

"Oh fuck," she gasped, already pathetically close.

Or maybe not so much pathetically, as timely.

They had spent a God-awful number of years on foreplay, and tonight . . . well, she might be naked, but they had spent more time talking than hurtling toward orgasm.

Though, that wasn't the case now.

He sucked and her head fell back, eyes unseeing as he pressed the flat of his tongue to the bundle of nerves, making her thighs clench instinctively around Graham's shoulders. Thank-fully, the forceful move on her part didn't dislodge him or deter his efforts.

Instead, he just clamped a palm on either knee, spread her wide, and redoubled his efforts.

Tongue circling, fingers sliding in and out.

All the while, she wound tighter and tighter and tighter . . . until he did something incredible with the tip of his tongue that had her gripping the edge of the desk, writhing against him, and—

Exploding.

Or that's what it felt like anyway. Her every nerve wound taut, threatening to snap and then they did—going suddenly loose and lax as wave after wave of pleasure flowed through her.

It was more tsunami that lapping swell, ripping through her, sending her adrift in the wide-open ocean before she finally found an anchor.

In Graham.

In his warm palms on her knees, in the gentle strokes of his tongue, the slightly roughened callouses on his fingertips.

In the way he coaxed her down from the peak, back into reality, and lightly cupped her cheek. His lips on hers were soft, a slight tang from her on his tongue as he trailed it lazily across hers.

Lazy kisses. Gentling.

Patience.

So much patience even though he was hard and pulsing against her stomach.

"Look at me, Firefly," he murmured.

She didn't even know that her eyes had slid closed. But something she *did* know? This tenderness, this gentleness wasn't fucking. This wasn't like any sex she'd ever had before.

This was more.

So terrifyingly, incredibly *more*.

Especially when she peeled back her lids and saw warm golden eyes, a soft smile on his face.

"I like making you come," he murmured.

Suz nibbled at the corner of her mouth. "I wish you didn't sound so cocky." She snaked her arms around his neck, held him close. "But I like it, too."

He chuckled, and the rasping sound coated her skin like chocolate syrup.

Which . . . if this happened a second time, she wouldn't mind licking off every inch of Graham's sexy-as-sin body.

A kiss that had her fantasies shoved away, that had her

gasping for breath, her thighs quivering, heat coiling in her abdomen again. Too quickly, considering she'd just had an orgasm that left her limp. But she wasn't feeling so limp after that kiss. Rather, she was trembling with need, already halfway to heaven, and aching to have him inside her.

His hands trailed over her body, down her throat, between her breasts, rubbing rasping palms over her nipples.

"I—"

But she didn't get more than that one syllable out before he'd captured one hard bud in his mouth, suckling deeply, taking her from halfway to heaven to nearly there.

Then he switched sides.

Fingers in his hair, hips bucking, pelvis nearly perfectly aligned to take him inside.

He chuckled, stilled her. "Not yet."

She might have been pissed that he was coherent, competent, in control, except that there were lines bracketing the sides of his mouth, sweat shining on his forehead, and every line of those long, lean muscles stood out in sharp relief.

He might be acting like they had all the time in the world.

But he was on edge, just as much as she was.

Hands sliding down from his shoulders, over his pecs, along the ridged muscles of his abdomen.

And then around his cock.

"Fuck!" he hissed, covering her hand when she stroked firmly. But he didn't brush it away again. He pumped against her, her falling forward, blazing eyes on his.

Hard, thick, tempting, and not inside her.

"Wait, Firefly. I want—"

But she kept stroking, unable to stop herself from running her hand over the velvet-covered steel. It felt so fucking good to be able to touch him like this, to be so close, to have her hands on him.

She shoved him back, dropped to her knees in front of him, her mouth—

"Enough," he rasped, tugging her back up, plunking her back atop the desk.

"Graham," she said. Or maybe it was a whimper. Either way, she was nearing that shaking, trembling edge again. She wanted to taste. She wanted him thrusting deep inside, moving fiercely.

He slid her forward on the desk, spreading her legs wider, his erection so fucking close.

And then he stopped.

Again.

She cursed. "Don't!"

Molten golden eyes on hers. "Birth control."

Was that all?

"I'm a fucking doctor," she snapped. "I'm covered."

"Good."

A wicked grin, one firm stroke, and he slid home.

Deep and hard and filling her so damned full. So damned good. So damned—

He moved.

And words became very difficult. This was . . . a flurry of sensation and pleasure—a whole *lot* of fucking pleasure. It was as though he'd opened her mind, reached inside, and plucked out every single urge and need and feeling. He knew what she required even before she recognized it herself. Pulling her closer, shifting the angle of her hips, thrusting a little harder.

Faster.

Yes. That was exactly what she needed.

"Graham," she moaned.

"So fucking pretty," he panted, his hips pistoning, his lips on her throat, her collarbone, swooping down to suck her nipple deep. "God, I've wanted you. I *want* you. I—"

He hit just the right spot, and she gasped, her breathing unsteady, too. Along with her mind being hazy, her vision reduced to pinpoints of light, her focus solely restricted to this man. Her senses only aware of the damp forest floor of his scent, the way he filled her so completely, how he was hard—so damned hard *everywhere*—and yet how he held her so, so carefully.

This was all she'd hoped for and dreamed about and . . . it was so much fucking *more*.

She'd expected good.

She hadn't expected *this*.

Panic and excitement. Pleasure and fear. And an ever-increasing pressure on the magic in the back of her mind.

Fingers on her clit. Lips on hers.

Heat coiling and tightening and—

Her orgasm barreled through her, exploding from her pussy, spreading outward. Every muscle in her was strung taut as that pleasure flowed over her for what might have been an eternity.

"Oh, fuck," she groaned. "Oh fuck. Oh *fuck*."

And Graham was still hard, still thrusting, still sending that orgasm sparking through her. As it subsided, she managed to peel back her lids. Then promptly lost her breath again at the intensity of his expression—sweat dampening the strands of his hair, his jaw clenched, eyes molten metal—

Then he followed her over the edge.

Golden eyes disappearing behind closed lids, his head falling forward to rest on her shoulder, hot breath glazing her skin, cursing—in a rasping, sexy voice that sent another pulse of pleasure through her—as he went limp against her.

But it was his hands that did it.

The way he held her hips, keeping them connected, drawing her close.

Gently.

Still so gently.

As though she deserved his care—and yes, part of her recognized that pathetic thought for what it was, pathetic, but the rest of her, the piece that had spent much of the last years alone, reveled in it.

Because that care was the key in the lock.

Later, she would wish it was just a proverbial lock, something made up of just pure fancy. Or perhaps the lock in her heart—and she supposed, in some ways it *had* to be in her heart, *opening* her heart—because as she sat there, perched on the edge of the desk in blissful stupor, soaking in the care, the feeling of right, the man who felt so fucking perfect deep inside her and . . .

The lock in her mind opened.

Her magic burst free.

Sparks coalesced into threads in the back of her brain. Those threads slid forward, down her spine, along her arms, out her palms, her fingertips.

A chocolate brown web of power surrounded her.

And then it surrounded Graham.

Before she could pull it back, shove it into the locked box in her brain adults used to contain their magic—because her powers shouldn't be free without her explicit control, it was what kept them safe and sane and—well, before *any* of that could happen, the golden threads of Graham's magic covered hers.

It was so pretty to see them like that. The colors went together perfectly, sparkling in the overhead light, almost as though she and Graham were the most unique and gorgeous statue of blown glass ever seen.

Then the filaments seemed to sink into one another, to weave together and . . . to become one.

One.

O.N.E.

Like—

Her orgasm haze faded.

Terror took the place of languid pleasure-laden limbs.

Because—

Her gaze flew to Graham's, saw the same shock on his face that had to be filling hers. Except hers was mixed with horror. Complete and absolute horror because it wasn't just that their magic was mixing or the odd chance of her losing control.

It was the space he'd created in her mind, her *heart*.

It was her ability to sense his emotions—enough for her to tell that he wasn't scared like she was. Instead, he was . . . pleased.

Really fucking satisfied.

"Firefly," he murmured, stroking his fingers over her cheek.

She let him because . . . well, shock and the aforementioned horror and—

Seriously? What in the absolute fuck?

Her hands lifted to his chest, shoved him back. She tried to hold on to the fear and fury. This wasn't right. This couldn't be. This—

Didn't make one fucking bit of sense.

"We've bonded."

FOUR

Graham

HE FELT SUZ'S FEAR.

Fear.

Fuck. Because fear wasn't what he was feeling. Rather, he felt as though a piece in his heart, a jagged, broken barb that had been stabbing him for an eternity, had finally been filed down.

Soothed. Made whole.

And the woman he was bonded to was fucking terrified.

She shoved at his chest again, and he backed up a step, trying not to focus on the fact that they were both naked, and he had just had the best sex of his life.

Sex wasn't important. Well, not *so* important.

Because he was bonded.

A magical, soul-deep connection to this woman—one that permanently linked them emotionally and mentally *and* magically.

The kicker?

If this bond wasn't nurtured, if they didn't navigate their

way to some sort of understanding and *happiness,* then their powers would disappear.

And they'd be human.

A fate scarier than death to a man who'd lived as long as he had.

But he couldn't worry about that now, not when the woman he had that fledging link with was terrified, fucking freaked out as she scrambled for her clothes and mentally distanced herself from him.

"This isn't r-right," she stammered. "This isn't—This *can't.*" Chocolate eyes found his. "This doesn't . . . it doesn't happen like this."

He reached for his underwear, tugged them on, repeating the process with his jeans. "It happened like this with Daughtry and Cody." A beat. "And Alex and John. And Gabby and Mason."

Fingers fumbling as she pushed back her hair. "They didn't know each other for decades. Not like us—" A sharp shake of her head. "They saw each other and *bam!* They were bonded."

It hadn't been quite that quickly, from what he'd heard from the Rengalla gossip train, but Suz was right. The other bonded couples hadn't spent decades knowing one another without a single inkling that there might be more between them—*more* being the potential of a magical connection that linked their minds and powers forever.

That was different.

But he wasn't going to look a gift horse in the mouth.

Because a mate was a gift.

And maybe he'd always kept his distance because deep down he'd known this would happen, maybe part of him had understood Suz for what she was to him and knew that if he would have gotten close, this would have happened, and he wouldn't have been able to bear letting her go off and find her feet.

Or maybe, Dee and Cody bonding had changed something, made it possible so the ritual, the connection his people had long thought dead, was able to make a reappearance.

Or maybe . . . he was wasting time thinking because Suz was fully dressed and taking off for the hall while he was standing there like a statue wondering about the grand schemes of the universe.

Dumbass.

He snagged his shirt and took off after her, tugging it over his head and trying not to notice the cold tile under his bare feet.

"Wait," he said, snagging her arm.

She shook him off, kept walking toward the door.

He grabbed her arm again. "Firefly."

"Fuck. Off," she snapped and though the words were sharp and caustic, the tone wasn't what stung. Instead, the riot of emotions—fear, terror, and horror—battered at his brain, nearly strong enough to make his eyes water.

"No," he snapped back. "We *have* to talk about this. Suz—"

She spun to face him, glaring at his hand where it was holding firmly to the top of her arm, and he felt a boiling anger rise up in her mind, moving toward him like a tidal wave. She opened her mouth—

A knock pounded on the door to the infirmary.

That anger banked immediately.

No, it wasn't quite banked, so much as locked behind a wall of calm. Mentally, he poked at that sheet of ice, able to see flickering flames of fury beyond it.

"Stop," she hissed, yanking her arm free, her mind shoving him out of hers.

Graham retreated, pulling back from her thoughts, not

because he or his magic wanted to, but because he was aware of exactly how gross an invasion of her privacy it was.

He was trespassing where he shouldn't.

Not intentionally, necessarily. The bond had opened up a channel.

But she didn't want him in her brain, so he shouldn't be there—even if every part of his body was telling him he should be ingrained on her mind, etched into her heart, permanently tattooed on every cell.

Which was crazy, he got that.

Thus was the power of bonding, he supposed.

"I'm sorry," he said, not touching her again but moving closer, crouching a bit in order to meet her eyes. "I didn't mean for this to happen."

That ice in her mind melting slightly. "I know. I'm sorry. It's just—"

The knock came again.

She jumped and winced. "I'm sorry," she said. "It could be—"

He slid past her, reached for the doorknob. "Don't apologize for doing your job," he told her. "It could be an emergency."

A blip in his mind—a grenade of emotion that exploded and splintered . . . and then that emotion was gone before he could process anything more than it was intense and laced with some deep-seated memories.

His eyes met hers.

"Please, just find out who needs help," she whispered.

He opened the door.

FIVE

Suz

THANK GOD FOR EMERGENCIES.

Emergencies of *this* sort anyway.

Because this one was solvable. This one would be finished in approximately twelve hours—or, if Felicia was lucky, a little less.

Today, her baby had decided to make an appearance.

"It's too early," Felicia said, gasping as another contraction had her huddling over.

Suz glanced at her watch. That was closer together than expected.

Only two minutes apart. From five minutes to two in—she looked at her watch again—under thirty minutes.

Okay, so this labor would probably be quite a few hours less than twelve.

Felicia cried out, grabbing tightly to the bedrail.

"It'll be okay," Suz told her, pushing away from the computer where she'd stepped away to log Felicia's information and moving quickly back to her side. "It's not too early. The baby measured large at your last appointment, remember?" She brushed the tear away. "He or she is ready to be held in your arms."

Felicia nodded. "But—"

"No, buts," Suz said. "You'll both be fine."

A tear slipped from Felicia's eye, and Suz had been through this exact scenario enough times to not be too worried. What Felicia was experiencing was a combination of nerves about the delivery (especially when it was moving this fast) and fear that she was going to actually be a new mom in reality and not just in her dreams.

"Promise?" Felicia asked.

"I promise," Suz told her.

"Okay," Felicia murmured. "Ok—*ow!*"

"Breathe, honey," she said, talking her through the contraction.

She groaned loudly, gripping the railing until it threatened to crack, until her knuckles were standing out in sharp relief. Hank, her husband, was lucky she had hold of that instead of his hand. "Oh God, it *hurts.*"

And it wasn't *all* nerves. It was also the pain.

Because this was fast. This labor was moving very fast, especially for a first baby.

"Lie back, honey," she ordered. "Let me see how things are going."

"Is it okay?" Felicia asked.

"Yes," Suz assured her. "I just want to see how things are progressing." She reached for Felicia's shoulder, coaxing her to lie back.

Then she looked.

And realized that fast had turned into warp speed.

She stood. "All looks good, honey. Just try to relax." Which Suz knew was easier said than done when she wasn't the one about to squeeze a watermelon out from a lemon. But it had to be said, especially because she needed a few things in place in order to safely bring this baby into the world.

She moved to the cabinet with her supplies, but before she could open it, Graham was by her side.

Discomfort trickled through the bond—the bond!—connecting them.

"Are you uncomfortable being next to me," she muttered. "Or because a baby's about to be born?"

"Neither," he said after a pause. "I'm uncomfortable because I don't know if Felicia is okay with me being in here. It's not like I know her that well, and this is an . . . intimate situation."

"Sounds like door number two," she said, standing on tiptoe to reach one of the birthing kits Gabby, her former receptionist and current nurse, had recently restocked. Speaking of which, "You called Gabby?"

He nodded. "No answer, but I left a message. I can go knock on her door, though." He reached past her, snagging the kit, his chest brushing her back, making her suck in her breath, making her *remember*. Making her remember too much when she was trying to pretend what had happened between them didn't *actually* happen. "Suz?" he said, when she didn't move. "Should I go get her?"

"No," she said quietly. "That'll take too long."

"Too *long*?" he hissed, lurching back.

"This baby is coming. Now."

"Shit."

"Yeah." She met his gaze. "And I'm out a nurse."

Now, the discomfort was related to a baby's imminent birth,

but the words that came out of Graham's mouth didn't align with the nerves she felt across their link.

"I guess I'm putting my first aid skills to use tonight."

Suz bit back a smile then her gaze caught on Felicia's husband, saw that Hank was a special shade of pale.

"Make sure he doesn't pass out," she said with a slight nod. "I don't need a second—or soon to be third—patient."

"On it," Graham said as she dragged a tray over and began laying out her supplies. "Sit," she heard him order, pushing Hank down into the chair next to the bed before asking Felicia softly, "Is it okay if I help Suz? Or do you want me to go?"

Felicia groaned again, head thrashing on the pillows. "Whatever gets this baby out sooner!"

A beat of amusement flicking from his mind to hers. "Suz is the expert on that. She'll make it happen, okay?"

She dragged a stool over, nodded to Graham. "Help me shift this bed." It only took him a minute to catch on, to mirror her movements so the gurney could be shifted into a birthing bed, and then he was carrying the removable panel to the side of the room while she was donning gloves and a gown before passing him a set to do the same.

Felicia, meanwhile, was squirming in pain. No matter how quickly Suz moved, having a baby was an agonizing business, especially Felicia's way—her birth plan called for a natural birth.

Still, Suz was a doctor and hated to see anyone hurting, especially when she could prevent it. She waited until the contraction ebbed. "Can I help you with the pain, sweetheart?"

"No," Felicia panted, sweat sheening her brow.

"Baby," Hank said. "You don't have to suffer."

"It's supposed to be like this!" Felicia declared. "I'm supposed to feel the baby, and if you take away the pain, I won't, and the drugs—" A shake of her head. "Something will go wrong and—"

"It's perfectly safe," Suz told her. "But I would never force you to do something you don't want."

"I—"

She moaned again, fingers finding Hank's, and Suz could swear she heard his bones creaking, though she struggled to find a whole lot of sympathy, regardless. A hurt hand wasn't exactly equivalent to pushing out a baby.

Making a mental note to pull an ice pack out of the freezer for him after the baby was safe and stable, Suz positioned herself to catch and glanced at Graham.

He'd pulled on the gloves and gown, was standing on Felicia's other side.

When he saw her looking, he nodded, mouthed, "You got this."

Funny how she'd never known that reassurance was something she craved. She'd spent so long making sure she could rely on herself, on not needing anyone else, on being so fucking untouchable that she could never be hurt.

And one positive affirmation melted her from the inside out.

"Ready to meet your baby, honey?" she asked Felicia.

"No." Felicia shook her head, eyes clamping closed, skin pale beneath the pink on her cheeks. "I'm not ready. I need—I need—" A groan. "I can't—it hurts."

Suz guided Felicia's heels into the stirrups. "Let me help you."

"No drugs."

"I know. *Felicia*." Suz waited until she opened her eyes, brought them to hers. "But I can help you without drugs." It was far too late for drugs at this point anyway, but she had something that normal doctors didn't have at her disposal.

Magic.

"Without drugs?" Felicia asked.

A nod.

It wasn't something Suz normally did, but frankly, she didn't normally get patients in this day and age that ended up with a natural birth. Most wanted epidurals, or if they started off wanting to be natural, a few hours of labor had them asking for relief.

Not that she blamed them.

But it just highlighted that Felicia's situation was different and moving fast and complicated.

And she needed to not be hurting.

"Yes," she said. "Without drugs. Are you okay with that?"

A nod. "Okay. Yes. Please."

Graham shifted down the bed, his gaze deliberately on hers. "What are you doing?" he whispered.

She ignored him. She was doing what she must.

Letting her eyes slide close, Suz focused.

Sparks of her power gathering into a ball in the back of her mind, readying to leave her body, to connect with Felicia's. But she nearly faltered when she realized it wasn't purely chocolate brown any longer, that it didn't match her eyes exactly. Instead, it was laced with gold.

With Graham's golden magic.

Panic swelled again, but she couldn't let it overwhelm her. Not when Felicia was hurting, not when she had a patient—patients—who needed her.

She was going to pretend she hadn't noticed.

She was going to compartmentalize like it was her fucking superpower.

And she was going to see this little baby brought into the world, to be held safely in the loving arms of two people she respected deeply.

Then she would continue freaking out.

And maybe commence drinking.

Slightly more settled, she was able to release a narrow thread of her magic, allowing it to crawl out of her mind to wrap around Felicia's ankle. She felt the skin, the muscles, the nerves beneath. Only once she was sure she was centered and fully in control did she allow it to crawl higher, up Felicia's leg to focus on her abdomen, then her womb. She could sense the baby—a boy, though the parents didn't know, since they'd wanted it to be a surprise. Moving deeper, keeping that tight grasp on her abilities, Suz concentrated until she sensed the muscles contracting.

There.

Because she'd also sensed the pain.

A whole huge wealth of it.

"Rest," she said, grabbing that pain, keeping the connection even as the hurt faded, as Felicia took a moment. "Breathe slow and steady and at the next contraction, get ready to push."

Felicia nodded, breathed, and though Suz was focused on her magic, on the baby, she heard Hank's encouragement, felt Graham shift back to Felicia's side, speaking softly.

Although, his focus was purely on her.

She could feel those gold eyes on her, his mind a sharpened bolt of attentiveness. But he kept out of her brain as she'd asked, continued to keep his distance and didn't press her for an explanation. Of course, that distance was in the form of as-much-as-he-was-able, because their link made it impossible for him to be truly separated. Which was why— insert more of her patented compartmentalization here—she was going to ignore the bond and its repercussions because this was real life and a baby was being born, and she needed to do the job she was trained for, the job that was written into her fucking DNA.

She was a healer.

Pure and simple.

As long as she had breath in her lungs and her heart was pumping, she would take care of her patients, her people.

Another contraction built, but this time Felicia wasn't alone.

Suz wrapped her magic around the pain and pulled.

What she felt began as a trickle, a slight prickle like a paper cut or stubbing a toe. But quickly it ramped up, her abdomen screaming, her teeth locking together as she absorbed Felicia's hurt.

Focus. *Focus.*

"That's it," she said, seeing the baby's head make an appearance. "That's a great push. Keep going." Her voice shook, throat tight, muscles locked, but neither Felicia nor Hank seemed to notice. Instead, Hank encouraged and bolstered, just as he should, and Felicia took a much-needed break.

Until the next contraction.

Then the same process repeated. Felicia pushing. Suz taking her pain. The baby descending.

But the third contraction felt different.

The baby was still making its approach, and Felicia was still doing a fabulous job of pushing, but the pain of the contraction she'd absorbed wasn't quite as intense as it had been on the two previous.

It was almost as if . . .

She flicked her eyes to the side.

It was almost as if someone was siphoning it off.

And she had a sneaking suspicion who.

Graham was still at Felicia's side, but instead of soft, reassuring words, he was ramrod stiff and silent.

More pain slid through her then disappeared off into that connection.

Off into Graham.

But before she could protest, before she could do anything

except process the heavy ache in her shoulders, the reverbera-
tion of the pain in her teeth, the baby was crowning.

Fast.

This little boy was going to end up an athlete or a teleporter
or fuck, something that was . . . speedy.

"Slow, now," she ordered. "Easy and breathe for a moment."

Felicia nodded, her dark hair stuck to her temples, her
cheeks still pink, her skin still slightly pale beneath it. But
instead of fear, there was determination. "Another is coming,"
she groaned, bearing down.

"Just a sec—okay," Suz said, clearing the baby's airway, slipping the tangled cord from around his neck. "Go ahead and
push."

Felicia pushed—like a fucking boss, if Suz did say so—and
before the contraction was winding down, the baby was born.
The adorable tiny munchkin with a scrunched-up face let out a
loud wail that had Hank letting out a relieved breath, Graham
relaxing, and Felicia crying softly.

It was one of those beautiful moments that made every hour
spent studying, every late night that pulled her out of bed and
into the infirmary worth it.

She wrapped the newborn up in a blanket and handed him
to Felicia then set about the less pleasant work of delivering the
placenta, taking care of the bleeding, and stitching a few
stitches. By the time she'd stripped off her gloves and thought
about changing the delivery bed back into a regular bed,
Graham was there with the pieces and they made short work of
getting Felicia and baby set up and cozy.

"Now," she said, once everyone was stable enough for her to
let down her guard for a few minutes, "you can go get Gabby."

Irritation—not hers—blared through her mind.

"Can I talk with you in the hall?" Graham gritted out.

A glance at the bed told her the family of three was fine, so she trailed him into the hallway.

But she'd barely gotten clear of the door before he pinned her against the wall.

"What in the fuck was *that?*" he snapped.

She shoved him back. "*That* was my fucking job."

Furious gold eyes. "How often?"

"What?"

"How often do you fucking put yourself through agony like that?" Her angry retort died on her lips at the chill lacing his words. "How often do you hurt yourself for someone else?"

"I—" She stopped, sucked in a breath and lifted her chin. "That's none of your fucking business. Now please, either leave or go get Gabby."

Fingers on her jaw, not quite gently holding her in place.

But not hurting her either.

Maybe that shouldn't have mattered when he was in her face and pissing her off by questioning her ability to do her job, but he was being careful with her.

Careful with *her*.

No one was careful with her. No one cared if she worked herself into oblivion.

And . . . truthfully, no one had noticed when she'd taken their pain before. Or at least, no one had ever asked her about it after the fact. But that was the point, wasn't it? She didn't take pain all the time—her body wouldn't be able to take a relentless push of agony day in and day out—she merely smoothed the edge, made it so they could breathe a little easier as she treated them. Only in the rare case of someone like Felicia, did she take on more.

"How often?"

Her chin remained in his grip. "As I said, that's none of your business," she whispered. "I'm nothing to you." Despite herself, her eyes drifted to the side, not able to hold his gaze.

"Not nothing."

Two words that she would have laughed at—if his magic wasn't currently living inside her.

She sighed, tugged her head free. "Graham, this doesn't—"

"You take anyone else's pain, you pass it to me," he said, or rather growled, not grabbing her again, but not stepping back either.

"I'm not—"

"You will let me help you," he said, still growling, still intense, and still making her feel like she was on a Tilt-a-Whirl. She'd known about bonding, obliquely anyway from the experiences of her friends, which meant that she knew it made the male part of the bond go a little cuckoo—protective, obsessive, domineering, and pushy.

But it was a whole other thing to experience all of that *maleness* herself.

To have it glaring down at her, surrounding her, pulsing against her mind.

And cue panic round seven million.

Which she was fully aware was hyperbole, but what was a woman to do without a little hyperbole every once in a while?

"Why?"

"Because you're mine."

Her breath shuddered out and she shook her head, not able to process the words. She had a job to do, so she really shouldn't be focused on the bond in her mind nor the fabulous sex nor the man whom she'd wanted to see her as she was. She certainly shouldn't be thinking that she'd fantasized about being this close to him for years, a teenaged crush morphing into the hope and awareness of an adult female who knew he would always be out of her league. And she couldn't be considering what it might be to have that very same man looking at her like she was important and valuable and—

His.

Like she was *his.*

She'd lived too long not being *anybody's* to just accept that at face value.

Even if she'd seen what bonding did to other couples, even if she understood it was intimate and rare and spectacular. *Fuck.* She couldn't think about it without wanting to hyperventilate and throw up.

Perhaps not at the same time.

Work.

She needed to focus on her work, on making sure Felicia and baby were happy and healthy and secure before she transferred the new mom back to her room to fully recover. Although —she made a mental note—she'd need to make sure the busybodies didn't intrude before they got settled. There was nothing the Rengalla loved more than a baby, and they'd be knocking on Felicia's door to cuddle the infant and ply Felicia with food, especially because things had been so tense of late.

In the midst of their people being betrayed, their enemy frequently at the doorstep, and then surviving attack after attack, including one that had nearly taken their home and everything their people had fought to survive, something as simple as wanting to hold a new precious baby was the joy that the Rengalla needed.

Just not at all once. Felicia needed rest.

"What are you thinking?"

The question was so soft that she forgot to be tense and on guard and actually answered it.

"That Felicia needs rest," she whispered.

The change over his face was stark—fury melting into gentle

—but not nearly as dramatic as the shift in his mind against hers. Respect, approval, and . . . pride.

He was proud of her.

But he didn't *know* her. Except . . . she supposed he *did* know her in many ways. She was friends with his sister, had been to many a family dinner, and she certainly knew him better than a stranger.

But deep down, he didn't know *her*.

Although the bond would make short work of any secrets she might want to hold on to.

Fuck, that was a scary thought.

"You're a good person, Firefly."

She shifted to the side, inching toward Felicia's room. "I'm just doing my job."

"And you say you're not a soldier."

She froze. "What?"

"You protect your people just like we do."

Her breath caught. "They're mine."

A brown brow lifted. "And you need to know that *you're* mine," he said in that silky tone that slid down her skin like honey and made her want to agree with anything he was saying.

"Graham," she began.

"So, you'll let me help."

Not that.

The fog cleared and she glared for a moment. Then sighed, abruptly exhausted. "I don't need your help." Another sigh, pushing back against the fatigue she knew was simply her adrenaline coming down. "Well, I'd love your help going to get Gabby, so I can get some sleep."

Fingers on her cheek, a small smile on that sexy mouth. "I'll go get Gabby."

"Great idea," she muttered. "I wish I'd thought of it—"

The sarcastic sentiment barely emerged before Graham's

lips were on hers, his tongue dipping inside her mouth, tempting her into forgetting her tiredness.

Because the man could fucking kiss.

But just as it really got started, as she was forgetting herself and where her body currently resided in the face of all that Graham power, he gently slowed the kiss, his lips slipping from hers. He cupped her cheek.

"I'll be right back."

Then he was gone, the door clicking closed behind him.

And she was alone in the hall of the infirmary, wondering what in the fuck had just happened to her life.

A whole hell of a lot, that was for damn sure.

SIX

Graham

HE STRODE down the hall to Mason's and Gabby's room, his mind spinning and alternating between wanting to smack himself around for bungling his interaction with Suz so badly and shock that his life had taken such a sharp left turn.

He wanted Suz.

Not just in bed.

And he was kicking himself for not having recognized that need sooner.

She . . . was incredible.

Though to be fair, he'd known that before. Or at least recognized she was a capable, smart woman. He'd even appreciated her beauty, her curves.

It was just that she was so much more.

Why hadn't he known she was so much more?

The door in front of him flew open, and truthfully, he hadn't even recognized that he'd stopped at Mason and Gabby's room, certainly hadn't noticed the crest of the LexTals —the symbol of the Rengalla's elite soldiers, higher than

Graham's own rank—on the wall outside their quarters. These rooms were marked to let a civilian know where to go if there was an emergency, and they'd also become a sort of open-door policy for anyone who needed assistance for anything big or small.

And Graham knew small could be *really* small.

He'd heard Mason complain just last week that someone had asked him to fix their leaking sink, and Tyler—another LexTal—had countered with his having been on tea party duty with the tiny five-year-old who lived a few rooms down.

But it could also be big.

Like a baby being born or news of an injury. It could even be someone informing them of an attack by the Dalshie.

Plus, big and small were both important.

Their people needed to have an outlet, a place to turn with issues, especially after what had happened with the former leaders of their people, The Council. Their elders had been infiltrated by their enemy, they'd turned to dark magic, and they'd nearly destroyed the Rengalla.

Cody, along with his bondmate, Daughtry, or Dee as she was more commonly known, and the other soldiers had managed to save the Colony and the Rengalla as a people.

Graham had helped a little.

He'd fought. He'd protected.

But the real star of the day had been Dee. Hell, she'd been the real star of the year, the century, the lifetime—if that was even a thing. Without her, they never would have taken the fight to the Dalshie, never would have struck out in order to protect their home. They simply hadn't had the power or insight to formulate such an attack.

She'd changed things.

And since then, any sign of surviving Dalshie had disappeared. They'd not come back to the Colony since that fateful day, and no one had seen a glimpse of them, anywhere in the world. But no one felt quite comfortable relaxing their guard.

The risk of dark magic hadn't disappeared.

So neither had the risk of more Dalshie.

Because the Dalshie *were* Rengalla—or had been at some point, until their magic had gone wrong and twisted, until they'd lost themselves to the temptation of power and cruelty. It began with a black stain on their right palm, crawling up their arm, and when it reached their heart, they were forever lost to humanity.

The only kind thing to do was . . . euthanasia.

A knife or bullet to the brain or heart and they were reduced to ash, to the elements the Rengallan magic was built on.

Maybe it sounded cruel, but there was no way out of the darkness, and many of their people had been slaughtered trying to convince themselves that some part of their loved one still existed in those monsters.

"You gonna say something?" Mason prompted, and Graham realized that he'd been standing there, lost in thought, for too fucking long. Mason's brows drew together, suspicion darkening his face. "Why do you look like that?"

Graham stiffened. "Like what?"

Hazel eyes narrowed. "Like . . ." And that was when Graham remembered that the bond wasn't just mental, but it was physical as well. If someone looked close enough, they'd see the magic coating his skin like a thin set of armor.

Only it wasn't just *his* magic—the color that matched his eyes exactly—it would also include strands of Suz's chocolate brown.

Like a blaring billboard indicating that he'd bonded.

"Gabby," he blurted before he could blurt something else.

Before he could blurt out the truth about the bonding.

Because he needed to talk to Suz first, needed to make sure she was . . . what? Okay with it? It wasn't like they had a choice. The magic had chosen and while they could rebuke the connection, he didn't think either of them wanted to live as a human. They both loved their people—

"*Graham.*"

He blinked. "What?"

Mason sighed. "Why are you at my door at three in the morning asking for my mate?"

"Suz needs Gabby," he managed.

"Why?"

Graham glanced down, realized that Gabby had appeared at Mason's side, a robe tied around her middle, hair askew, and eyes tired.

"What is it?" she asked.

Now was the time to get his shit together.

And remarkably, he was finally able to clear his mind enough to meet Gabby's eyes and say, "Felicia had her baby."

The tiredness disappeared from her face, and she gaped. "What?" she asked, turning away and going to the armoire on the far side of the room. She yanked out some clothes then crossed back to him. "Why did no one come and get me?"

"There wasn't time," he said, averting his eyes when she reached for the tie of her robe.

"*What?*" she said on another gape. "What do you mean there *wasn't time?*"

"Wait," Mason muttered to him, shutting the door in his face, and rightfully so. Graham didn't want to see her change.

Not because Gabby wasn't pretty.

She was.

But she was Mason's, and . . . she wasn't Suz.

He listened to the mumble of their voices and in a remarkably short time, Gabby had emerged into the hall, jeans and a sweatshirt having replaced the robe, and sneakers on her feet.

"There wasn't time?" Gabby asked again.

"The baby was born not long after Felicia and Hank knocked on the infirmary door."

"Whoa. How far apart were the contractions when she showed up?"

He shrugged.

"Right," she said. "Why would you know?"

Another shrug.

Shaking her head, she kissed Mason on the cheek and turned away from them, hurrying down the hall.

"You played catcher?"

Mason's question took him by surprise. "What?"

"You catch that baby?" A smack on his arm. "Heaven help you if you dropped it."

"Hilarious," he muttered. "First, it's a boy, not an *it*, and second, it's not like either of us hasn't seen more than a few babies born in our time."

Mason shuddered. "And it's not something I want to repeat."

It wasn't exactly on Graham's list of favorite things to do, either, but there was something magical—no pun intended—about seeing new life come into the world. "I didn't think you were such a wilting flower."

"Wilting flower?" Mason snorted.

"Yup."

"How old are you?" Mason asked.

"Old enough," he muttered, "as you well know."

"Mmm," Mason said. "Something else I *know* is that pattern of magic I can see on your skin. Something to share?"

Fuck no.

Especially when the woman he'd inexplicably bonded with was panicking anytime she remembered they'd forged the connection. He needed time to process—or rather, he needed time for Suz to process because he'd decided that she was *his*. His magic had taken matters into its own hands—or maybe his subconscious. Regardless, he'd also decided that she needed someone to look out for her, and the someone to do that was going to be him.

He would make sure she didn't work too hard, didn't take pain from her patients (and if she did, he'd take it from her, the stubborn woman).

He'd ensure she didn't skip meals and got enough sleep.

He would kiss her and hold her and make her understand that she deserved someone who would care for her.

But . . . what if she didn't want him?

He felt like the bond had simply unlocked the door, pushed it wide, eliminated any of the concerns and reservations he'd had for keeping his distance. He suddenly didn't give two fucks that she was his sister's friend or younger than him.

He *wanted* her.

Now he was worried that she didn't want him, that the sudden connection forged in the heat of the moment would be unwelcome.

And they'd be stuck with it.

She'd be stuck with him, if she wanted to keep her magic.

Fucking hell. Suddenly, he felt sick, nausea burning the back of his throat, his stomach churning.

Because he'd been arrogant enough to not consider that possibility.

Of course, considering it had been less than two hours since he'd bonded with Suz, there was probably a shit-ton of angles he hadn't considered. Which was all the more reason to get back to her, to make sure she wasn't panicking and distancing herself and—

Enough.

He needed to get the fuck out of his head and back into reality.

And Suz.

To Suz. Not *in*. Not that he didn't want *in*. It was just—

"Nothing to say for yourself?" Mason stepped close and swiped a hand down Graham's arm, fingers dancing through the magic coating his skin. "Because this is big news. *Big* news everyone is going to be *dying* to hear about. Who, I wonder," he asked, eyes dancing as he tapped his lips, "has chocolate brown eyes?"

Graham sidled away. "I'm going to make sure Gabby got to the infirmary—"

"She has."

"How do you know?" Graham glanced over his shoulder at the man who'd he thought was his friend. *Was* because that same man was currently looking way too fucking smug. He knew, the bastard, and he'd tell his brothers, and then *everyone* would know.

When their eyes met, Mason tapped his temple. "I *know*."

Ah.

The whole telepathic connection thing.

He tried to regain some of the conversational power—read: blackmail material. "Gabby know you go all sniffer dog on her?"

Mason didn't lose his smirk. "Gabby knows that it's impossible for me to *not* know her whereabouts, at least somewhere in my subconscious, when we're this close. It's"—he shrugged —"just . . . she's my heartbeat."

His heartbeat.

Fuck.

Longing rose within him. Graham wanted *that*. Wanted to be there with Suz. Wanted the uncertainty to be gone and for them to be settled—

After two hours.

Yeah, he knew that was unreasonable.

But for all his self-control, he wasn't a patient man. When his mind was made up, he wanted what he'd chosen.

And he'd chosen Suz.

Or his magic had—

No. That wasn't right. He'd chosen to take that inevitable step from the moment he'd followed her into the infirmary. He'd wanted her and even though he'd kept his distance, tied all of the feelings and emotions and needs down, burying them deep enough they'd never escape, something had shifted that night.

Now his need was out in the open.

"You don't have to look so miserable," Mason said. "Suz isn't all bad. Sure, she likes to bust balls, but—"

Graham had moved even before he realized it. He must have blacked out or something because one second, he was escaping the LexTal's presence and the next, he had Mason pinned against the wall, hand wrapped around the other man's throat.

"Don't talk about her like that," he snapped. "Suz is—"

But he broke off when Mason began laughing, a shit-eating expression on his face. "Man, you got it bad."

"Fuck off," Graham muttered, releasing the asshole and striding away down the hall.

"Tell me again why you aren't a LexTal?" Mason called.

Graham just flipped him off.

The truth was that Dante, the leader of the LexTals, had asked him to join the ranks of the elite soldiers many times over the years, but Graham . . . well, Graham's mother wouldn't have been able to handle him being away that much.

The LexTals cycled out of The Colony on regular intervals, checking on their people who lived on their own, helping humans—secretly—and hunting down any remaining Dalshie.

They were on the front lines and at the most risk, and he'd known his mother wouldn't have been able to handle him gone that much, would have worried herself into an early grave if he did accept the position.

She wasn't strong like Suz.

He loved his mom, but she was . . . fragile.

She could barely tolerate him being a senior soldier, as it was. She'd positively freak if he suddenly became a LexTal.

But then again, the Dalshie threat had been neutralized— or at least, they *thought* so. Everyone was still on edge, even though it had been a few months since the final attack, since the Rengalla had decided to take the fight to the Dalshie, successfully eliminating every enemy they knew of. The trouble was that they couldn't be sure they'd gotten all of them.

There could be more, and they could be out there, regrouping in their quest to hunt down every Rengalla on the planet.

"Tell Suz hi for me," Mason called just before Graham turned the corner.

Fuck.

"Also, that second skin of yours should fade in no time."

"Shut up."

"Really," Mason said loudly. "No one will notice. I'm just very observant and—" Graham turned around, narrowed his eyes. "What?"

"You're a fucking pain in my ass."

"That's the nicest thing you've ever said to me."

Graham could swear the fucker fluttered his eyelids, and just because he could—and also maybe because he couldn't stand the cat-ate-the-canary expression on Mason's face—he flicked his magic.

Just the slightest flip of air magic.

Just enough to push Mason's foot when he turned and started to go back inside his rooms.

Just enough to make the dumbass stumble over a solid block of air . . . that disappeared even as Mason tripped. Unfortunately for Graham, Mason had two brothers who were notorious for their mischievousness *and* Mason was well-trained and quick on his feet. Which meant he didn't land flat on his face as Graham had hoped.

He did look like he was attempting to dance a very awkward dance, at least for a few seconds.

So at least that was something.

"Fuck you, Graham!" Mason hollered.

"You're not my type," he yelled back. "Not pretty enough."

SEVEN

Suz

HE WAS STANDING THERE.

Staring.

As if she didn't feel him blaring in the back of her mind, driving her absolutely crazy as she tried to finish her work. She was tired and wanted to sleep, but Graham was propping up the wall outside her office—not intruding in a physical sense, or at least not crossing the threshold.

Just standing there.

Waiting.

Patiently.

Yes, she'd said that correctly.

Patiently.

A feeling she could be absolutely certain of because he was in her *mind!* Just hanging out there, a warm glow, a masculine presence waiting in both the mental and physical realms.

And again, not impatiently.

She couldn't remember a time *anyone* had waited for her to

finish her charting patiently, most of all a man who clearly wanted to speak with her.

But there was no sighing or foot tapping, nor any annoyed shifting of body language.

He just stood there.

And waited.

What in the ever-loving fuck was she going to do?

Especially as her work was taking about ten times longer than it should have because she kept glancing up to confirm he hadn't moved—he hadn't, not since he'd traipsed into the infirmary about five minutes after Gabby. It also didn't help that her mind kept probing at his presence in the back of her brain—also reassuring (ugh, reassuring!) herself that he hadn't moved.

Which, of course, she'd firmly established he hadn't and wasn't likely to and—

"You're like a tiny tornado in my brain," Graham murmured, speaking for the first time, making her jump and nearly sending her clinging to the ceiling.

She tore her eyes away from where she'd been admiring the way his T-shirt settled over his pecs, emphasizing his strength without being too tight. Considering she'd kissed her way across that chest not too long before, had been held against the planes of his body, been lifted so easily into his arms, she considered herself an expert on the proper way to display that chest.

And she approved it being displayed via snug-fitting cotton.

A curl of amusement in her mind.

Not from her own brain.

Her eyes flew to his, to the golden irises now sparking with humor . . . and with knowledge.

Knowledge that he'd known what she was thinking.

"I'm a fan of snug-fitting cotton myself," he murmured into the bond—was it even possible to murmur so silkily and sexily into a mental connection? Regardless if it were

possible or not, the man had done it, and his voice was so crystal clear in her brain that she would have sworn he'd spoken aloud.

Except it was more intimate, as though the words were brushing along the inside of her skin.

"How?" she said. "How did this happen?"

Misery and joy in equal measures slid through her.

She couldn't possibly be what this man wanted—*whom* he wanted to be tied to for an eternity. And that wasn't some self-loathing bullshit. Suz knew she was smart and capable and reasonably pretty, even though she didn't consider her attractiveness as something that added to her worth. Graham had avoided her—and *her* in particular—for some unknown reason over the years, and now he was saddled with her, if they both wanted to keep their magic.

Which, of course, they did.

Or at least, she assumed he did.

Because she certainly couldn't imagine being without her ability to heal. Something inside her would curl up and die.

It—

Fingers on her cheek.

She didn't jump this time, even though she hadn't sensed him move. Or maybe she had, but because he was in her mind, it just seemed normal?

It was all so confusing and overwhelming, and she was a woman who didn't get overwhelmed or confused—or panicked or uncertain—but hell if she didn't feel all of that in this scenario.

What was she going to do?

"Come on," Graham said.

"What?" she murmured.

"Your mind is too scattered for you to have any hope of getting more work done tonight," he said gently then smiled.

"But I can keep standing here silently until you decide you've had enough."

"I've had enough," she muttered.

He lifted a brow.

"Of you."

He grinned, tugged a strand of her hair. "I *can* be rather annoying."

She laughed. Despite herself, she laughed. Also, *dammit.* Because she was trying to be miserable and panicked and she shouldn't be laughing, not when her life had changed so dramatically in the last couple of hours.

"Come with me," he asked again, straightening and leaning his hip against her desk, and she couldn't ignore that she felt the words in her mind as well as heard them aloud.

"I should finish this."

"You should get some sleep, and then you'll be able to get through this all that much quicker."

Suz made a face. "I'm not tired."

Which wasn't exactly true. Frankly, she was exhausted, bodily anyway. Her mind was racing, and she knew it wouldn't stop, even if she was prone on her mattress. Instead, she would spend hours in bed, staring at the ceiling, the weight of all the outstanding charting she had left to do sitting on her chest and making it impossible to get some meaningful rest.

"Fine," he said. "But come with me anyway." He shifted closer, the damp earth scent of him reminding her of the forest and how long it had been since she'd hiked.

She missed that.

Being outside. The cool breath of wind on her cheeks. The sun shining down from above. Watching that giant ball of gas set in the distance, the sky trading bright blue for reds and oranges and yellows, and then eventually for navy, for black as the stars overhead made an appearance.

Lately, it had been a combination of too dangerous and too much work for a Rengalla to venture outside the Colony—or outside the shield, anyway.

That shield was made of Bond Magic, a tangle of rainbow-colored threads that their enemy was hard-pressed to penetrate.

But now, their enemy was vanquished.

Or mostly, it seemed.

The last insurgence had been just under three months before. The Dalshie making a take-or-break, no-holds-barred assault on the Rengalla. They'd gotten through the shield, hurt several of their people critically, and then . . . Daughtry. She was just a girl, reed-thin and so damned young. But she had *power*. And that power had bested their enemy, reduced them to ash, to nothing.

And their people were finally safe.

Or at least, that was what everyone hoped. They'd all been too terrorized for too long to truly let their guard down.

"Suz?"

"It's not safe."

Steady gold eyes on hers. "I'll keep you safe." A beat. "And we'll stay inside the shield."

"It's late and cold," she hedged.

A wolfish smile. "I'll keep you warm."

"I shouldn't."

"This might be our last chance to avoid the gossip train for a good long while," he pointed out.

Quite rightfully.

So . . . she caved. It was probably stupid, but he was being so nice, and she'd liked him for so long, and he'd been so good and patient with her work—not to mention he hadn't freaked out about being part of her baby delivery team.

Well, he *had* freaked out.

But not about the new life entering the world. Instead, he'd gotten furious about her taking the pain, but she couldn't exactly call that freaking out.

About the baby anyway.

It was also—and she wouldn't admit this out loud—nice to have someone focus on her for a change, to want to spend time with her alone. Sometimes she felt like a piece of furniture. A steady hall table, perhaps, a solid piece of wood that was always there at the ready to hold one's keys.

And now, she was being ridiculous.

A table, really?

Good grief.

She was losing it, and maybe that was the strongest reason to get away from her desk. Her work might not be completed properly if she continued on like this. She could mix up a patient's chart or mess up with treatment or—

She could just admit that she wanted to spend time with Graham.

However stupid that might end up proving.

Because she couldn't shake the feeling that this was all going to implode in her face and—

"Stop thinking so hard, Firefly," he whispered, stepping close.

It was more gentle encouragement than order, and for that reason, she found she could obey.

She pushed out of her chair.

"Okay," she told him. "Let's go see this thing you're desperate to show me."

He smiled and it felt like sunshine on a dark day, warming her from the inside out, filling her with hope and—

Old trajectories were hard to ignore.

Because she found herself adding, rather unkindly, she was fully aware, "I just want to get it over with."

EIGHT

Graham

HE CHUCKLED, not in the least bit put off.

Her words might be sharp.

But her mind wasn't.

So no, he wasn't hurt—not that he was the type of man to get his feelings hurt from a simple snapped out statement. He'd been on this planet long enough to understand some portion of behavior, even that of the mysterious feminine variety. Which meant he understood that though Suz was trying to put some distance between them, it wasn't because she wanted him to go.

She was a wounded animal, cornered and scared.

He understood why she felt cornered—he felt a little penned in himself with the whole permanent mental connection situation they had going. What was more concerning was why she felt scared.

Simply because of the bond?

Or something more?

Something . . . deeper?

Graham was leaning toward deeper. Mostly because he'd never

seen Suz scared, especially when faced with a challenge. And yes, he was chalking the bond up to a challenge. It had been thrust upon them, a winding course they needed to figure out how to navigate together, and not one either of them had been prepared to traverse.

"Come on, Firefly," he said, snagging her hand and leading her from the office. She'd said she'd come with him, but he had no doubt she'd try to delay or even to decamp.

"I need to check on Gabby and Felicia."

"We're good," Gabby chimed in, sticking her head out of the patient room, which was perfectly impeccable timing as far as Graham was concerned.

"I—" Suz began.

"You need sleep," Gabby pressed. "Go get some."

"But—"

"Remember that whole mandatory five hours of rest thing you implemented?" Gabby asked, eyes dancing as she glanced from their interlaced hands up to Graham's face. "It was *mandatory*, and," she added, voice dropping, "for the good of our patients."

Suz sighed, knowing when she'd been bested. "You'll do a visual check on mom and baby every twenty minutes. Perform a physical check on Felicia before she leaves—which shouldn't be sooner than a few hours—though she's more than welcome to stay as long as she wants."

Gabby smiled. "She's already asked for her own bed."

"That's fine with me," Suz told her. "In a few hours."

"Got it." Gabby nodded. "I'll follow the protocol—"

"And call me if there are any issues?"

"And call you if there are any issues," Gabby confirmed, nodding again, more firmly. "Now go . . . have fun, enjoy your private time before the rest."

"Gabby!"

"Oh and don't worry, that magic coating your skin like glitter from a strip club will fade before long." She paused, glanced back at them, chirping, "Though not before you're a blazing billboard for every single Rengallan that you belong to Graham."

Suz stiffened.

Graham tugged her toward the door. "Don't give her the satisfaction," he said, whispering softly in her ear.

"She'll be satisfied either way," she muttered.

He glanced down at her, lifted a brow.

"She's been wanting me to be felled by a man for ages."

"And are you?" he asked.

"Felled?"

He nodded.

"No."

"Hmm."

"I'm not."

He opened the door. "Of course not," he told her. "We've been bonded for what"—he glanced at his watch—"all of six hours? That hasn't given me much time to fell you."

A blip of emotion in his mind.

No, *panic* in his mind.

Graham wanted to grasp on to that emotion, to delve deep into the meaning beneath it, but every instinct inside him told him that would be a mistake, so instead of acknowledging her fear, he just slipped his hand from hers, wrapped his arm around her shoulders, and pulled her against his side.

"Come on, Firefly," he whispered. "It won't be *that* bad."

"The gossip?"

"No," he said and chanced pressing a kiss to the top of her head. Pleasure rolled through him when she didn't push him away, even after he said, "That'll be worse than bad."

She glanced up with narrowed eyes and this time, he couldn't resist pressing a kiss to that pretty mouth.

"No," he told her when he'd pulled back. "It won't be that bad spending time with me."

Suz froze, lips parting and tempting him again.

Then she laughed, and the warm sound filled an empty place inside him he hadn't even known existed.

And he had to kiss her again.

Lush lips against his, warm laughter coating his tongue, strong fingers sliding up his chest to grip his shoulders. Breasts against his chest, her scent in his nose, and her soft moan rising up her throat to collide with his. Kissing her was . . . coming home. They fit perfectly together.

"Graham," she whispered. "I . . ."

He waited to see if she'd finish her thought, and when she didn't, he ran his thumb over her bottom lip. "Let me show you?"

The potential, the future, the silly spot he'd wanted her to see, he wasn't sure which of those he actually wanted in the moment. But he did know what was most important.

Right now.

This moment.

She sighed, leaned against his side. "Okay, Graham. Just . . . okay."

"Great." Then just because he could, he kissed her once more.

"Was that what you wanted to show me?" she asked, her eyes dancing, her body and mind finally relaxed against him.

"No," he admitted.

She chuckled. "Well, as you may know," she murmured, breasts brushing against his chest, fingers dancing along the waistband of his jeans—and his body responding predictably, "I don't mind you showing me *something*."

He caught her hand just as it cupped the hard length of him.

Note, he really didn't *want* to catch it, and he sure as shit didn't want to pull it away. But as much as he wanted to show her *something*, he was following his instincts with this, and his instincts told him that turning to the physical—even though he wanted her with an intensity that was bordering on desperation, especially considering it had barely been any time at all since he'd had her last—would be a mistake.

They'd gone at this backwards.

They needed to learn each other, take some time where they weren't getting naked and coaxing pleasure from each other to figure out what this all meant.

Even though desire was coiled inside him like a cobra ready to strike.

He quite possibly had never wanted anything more than he wanted this woman, and once certainly hadn't been enough, especially with the bond telling him that he should get her naked and just orgasm any of her fears away.

But that wasn't what she needed.

"Come on, Firefly," he said, snagging her hand and holding it safely tucked into his side.

Then the other one, when she decided to put that one to good use.

"Behave," he grumbled.

She smirked, and he felt the bolt of self-satisfaction tickle across his mind, but she didn't fight him as he walked her along the hall. "Why do you call me that?"

"Call you what?"

"Firefly."

"Hmm."

"Graham," she hissed, smacking him lightly.

At least she wasn't reaching for his cock again, because as

good as it felt for her to touch him, he was on edge and the bond was pulsing in the back of his mind, coaxing him to claim, to touch, to get her naked again and make *all* the tiny Rengalla babies.

Fuck, he'd heard from the gossip train that bonding turned a reasonable man into a possessive dog protecting its bone, but he'd never expected to be in the position, to have a bondmate, so he'd never expected to be feeling this . . . full body urge to claim, to protect, to scream to the world that this woman belonged to him. And that he belonged to her right back.

Even though it had been mere hours.

She was . . . *it*.

He knew that with all certainty. He knew it like the sun was the center of the solar system and that there were twenty-four hours in the day. He knew it like he'd known he'd had to keep his distance so she could grow up and find herself. He knew it like he knew he'd been kidding himself in thinking that he'd actually be able to keep that distance, knew it like how he'd tried and failed to use his sister as a shield.

And he knew it like he knew that this had always been inevitable, that even though he'd been doing his best to stay away, his resolution to do so had been slowly chipping away.

Until he'd given in.

Until he'd seen that she needed him.

She. Needed. Him.

So, he couldn't turn away.

Suz cleared her throat, and he realized she wasn't going to let him off the hook, that she was going to demand an explanation for the nickname.

Maybe he could kiss her until she forgot about the line of questioning.

"No," she said, "you couldn't get me to forget."

He blinked. "What?"

She tapped his temple. "Bond, remember? I heard that thought," she told him.

"It's not supposed to be that strong yet." Bonding made the initial connection, but it was supposed to take time for them to be able to read each other clearly enough to pick up stray thoughts. From what he understood, it was supposed to begin as an impression of feelings, and only as the bond deepened did it grow to something more telepathic.

"Well, strong or not," she said with a shrug. "I heard that one loud and clear."

"What else have you heard?"

A frown. "Not much really. Just your mind in the back of mine, the odd stray emotion." She slid a glance in his direction, a shy smirk. "Mostly desire."

He slid his palm up and down her arm. "Can you blame me? You're gorgeous."

"You certainly gave no indication that you were attracted to me over the years," she grumbled. "And yes, I know you say it's because I'm friends with Amelia, but—"

"But what?"

"But . . . there has to be something more."

"Suz," he began.

"You can tell me," she murmured. "If you don't want this, I understand. It's not like either of us planned this or really wanted—"

He tugged her to a stop. "Don't finish that sentence."

Her eyes narrowed. "Don't order me around."

"Then don't say idiotic things." Graham cupped her jaw. "You're much younger than me, Firefly. Young and innocent, and I didn't want to take any of that time away from you."

"What time?"

"The time to be you. The time to strike out on your own and figure out the person you wanted to be in this world." He brushed his thumb along her skin, reveling in the silk of her skin. "I couldn't intrude on that."

She paused. "And so, you stayed away?"

"Well," he said. "It was made a little easier when you left for school."

"I've been back for decades," she pointed out. "If it was so difficult for you to resist me, you'd think that you would have made a point to reach out to me before now. I'd certainly"—she lifted her fingers, made air quotes—"*found myself* by then. And no, you couldn't kiss me and make me forget that point." She rolled those pretty brown eyes. "You're not *that* good of a kisser."

"Now, that sounds like a challenge," he said, spinning them around and trapping her against the wall. They weren't that far from their destination, but he couldn't let such a sentiment stand.

"It's not a—"

His mouth dropped to hers, tongue slipping between her lips, teasing hers out to dance with his, and though they were in the middle of a corridor, though anyone could stumble upon them and see this—the proverbial cat escaping the bag—Graham didn't quite have the strength to stop.

Or couldn't summon up any reason to, anyway.

Not with her fingers slipping beneath his T-shirt, tracing over the skin on his back, sending rivulets of desire through his body. No instead, he wanted to strip off his shirt and let her touch him anywhere—or kiss him.

Either way, he did have enough control to keep his hands on the wall and not on those sexy curves of hers.

Because if he touched her curves, if he let his control slip that far, he'd strip her naked in this corridor and really give the gossip train something to talk about. He almost didn't care. He almost lifted his hands from the smooth plaster of that wall. He almost—

Fuck.

He yanked his lips free, breathing heavy, their breaths painting each other's mouths, hers sweet and with a tinge of coffee making him want to close that half inch, to kiss her all over again.

By some herculean ability, he managed not to.

Stepping back and tucking her to his side again, he guided her back in the direction they'd been walking.

"Why, Graham?" she asked quietly, tentatively, and maybe he might have made a joke or kissed that tempting mouth again if he hadn't felt her mind curled carefully in the back of his, cautious and . . . preparing herself, like she expected him to say something that would hurt her.

"I don't know, sweetheart," he admitted. "It's just . . . I spent so long pretending that I didn't feel anything for you and somehow, it almost became the truth. Like it was bundled so deep that I truly didn't feel anything."

Her breath caught.

"Then you looked at me in the hall, invited me—*no*." A sharp shake of his head. "No, I think the veneer began peeling back when I saw you after the attack. You were so strong and unwavering. I was so fucking proud that I knew you, even obliquely." He laughed and just let the rest of it flow. "I knew you had a date last night, and some perverse part of me wanted to torture myself. So I came by, preparing to punish myself, thinking he would be smart enough to recognize how great you were, even though I knew I couldn't have that for myself."

"I-I don't understand."

"And even though I expected him to grab on to the wonderful woman in front of him—to you," he said, pulling her closer, "part of me hoped he would be dumb and that you would be there by yourself. Waiting for me."

"I—"

"I've watched you there," he murmured. "Watched you go into the infirmary at all hours of the night and not emerge for days."

"I—"

He placed a finger on her lips. "I've seen you working so fucking hard. You're amazing and inexhaustible, and just I respect all you're doing and have done for our people. First and foremost, you need to know that." He removed his finger, nudged her forward. "Second, you're the smartest person I know"—she snorted, and he bopped her on the nose with his pointer finger—"it's true. And last in this particular list, but not last in the things I like about you list, you're beautiful." A beat. "But even though I want to lick every inch of your sexy little body, I want you more than just in my bed."

Her chest was rising and falling rapidly, but this time when he stopped for air, she didn't try to say anything.

Instead, she was silent, just breathing.

Silently.

"Suz?"

She waved a hand, which he took to be her saying wait a moment.

So he waited and walked.

Then waited some more.

And then just when he was bursting with the need to say something, *anything* she turned to him, stopping him in his tracks as she wrapped her arms around his waist and squeezed tight.

"That's a lot," she murmured against his chest. "A lot that means . . ." Her breath caught. "Probably more than it should." She shifted, resting her forehead against him.

"But it's still a lot," he said.

She nodded, her ponytail going askew as she did so. "Yeah."

"So we stop worrying about the *a lot*, and we look at what I wanted to show you." He threaded his hand into her ponytail. "Then you get some sleep." Tugging gently, he waited until her gaze came to his. "And *then* when you wake up, this all won't feel like a lot any longer."

One half of her mouth curved. "How do you know?"

"Because I'm older and wiser."

A snort, but the uncertainty in her eyes had faded. "I'll give you older." She lifted her chin in the direction he'd been leading her. "You gonna show me this secret spot, or what?"

"What."

She rolled her eyes. "Seriously?"

He grinned. "I like teasing you, Firefly."

"When are you going to tell me what that means?"

"When I feel like it." He waggled his brows. "Or when you convince me to give up the goods."

"Graham!"

He just grinned.

And then he kissed her again, thoroughly and quite desperately.

"Now?" she asked when they broke apart.

"Nope," he said lightly, straightening and taking her hand again.

Her annoyed huff was the best sound he'd heard all day.

NINE

Suz

OKAY, it was worth the walk.

But maybe not the kisses.

Which was a lie, she knew. The kisses had been . . . incredible, more than she'd ever imagined. More than she'd ever *hoped*, truthfully.

A finger tapped her temple. "Still a tornado in there," Graham murmured.

Yeah, she did have a tornado in her mind, but she was putting that aside for a moment. Because he had taken her outside. *Outside.* Outside to a tiny little slice of nature, one that had become few and far between since the Dalshie's attack had destroyed a large portion of their outdoor space.

What had once been a beautiful expanse of trees and walking paths had been reduced to nothing more than splinters of wood and dirt.

They were rebuilding, slow and steady, but it would take ages for it to be what it was.

And she missed it.

She missed walking the trails after a tough day or a tough patient or a tough injury. She missed *this*.

Cool air on her skin, the soft rustle of leaves on the trees.

"How did you do this?"

Graham nudged her forward out the doorway, and she stepped out on the small patio. "I grew it."

"But how?"

His front came very close to her back. "With soil and sunlight and seeds."

She snorted. "You know that's not what I mean."

"It's my place," he said with a shrug. "I come here to be alone."

"You're not alone now," she pointed out.

He grinned. "Funny how that works. Although," he added, "one might be able to say that *we're* alone."

"Hmm. Is that right?"

Slightly roughened fingers brushed back the hair from her forehead. "That's right."

Her breath caught when those fingers slid lower, tracing the shell of her ear, drifting down her throat. "What's your favorite flower?"

She giggled. "Really?"

A shrug. "Seems like something I should know."

"Peonies."

"Noted." A beat. "You're not going to ask what my favorite is?"

"Do you have a favorite?"

He nodded at the lights hanging in the pair of trees filling the small space, highlighting the pots of plants overflowing with brightly colored flowers below. "Yes."

She waited. "And what's the answer?"

"Woo me, and I might just tell you."

Giggles burst out of her. "You're incorrigible, you know that, right?"

"I may have been told that a time or two," he said, lips tipped up at the corners. "Come here." He laced their fingers together, tugged her toward a large basket in the corner. A moment later, he'd snagged a brightly patterned cushion from inside it and set it on the dirt-covered ground. Then he extracted a blanket.

"What are you doing?" she whispered.

"I'm trying to watch the sunrise and hang out with my bondmate."

For some reason, that made her smile. Maybe it was the space or the cushion and blanket. Perhaps it was just spending time with Graham, who despite the torrent of emotions he evoked in her, also made her feel . . . settled?

That might be the only way she could think to describe it.

As scary as the thought of having someone so close was, Graham somehow managed to sand down the rough edges inside her, to fill in those jagged pits that took up so much fucking space in her heart. She wasn't quite so empty when she was with him. So, if she wasn't thinking about the whole way her life had changed in just one moment—cue another rapid rise in blood pressure—she actually felt sort of nice. Fine. More than nice or fine actually, but regardless of precisely *what* she felt, in that moment Suz decided she was going to turn off her brain and just enjoy the time with him.

Later, she could worry about the rest of it.

Tonight—or well, this morning, she could just live in the freaking moment.

Which was why she let him coax her down onto the cushion, why she didn't shift away when he sat down next to her, his side pressed to hers, his thigh flush and strong and hot.

Or maybe that was just Graham—warm and strong and hot.

"You think I'm hot?" he asked, grinning down at her.

"Stop cherry-picking my thoughts!" she exclaimed.

More grinning, the smug asshole.

"I think my smugness is warranted," he said, slipping his arm around her shoulders. "And I'll talk to Cody and Mason as soon as I can to figure out a way to shield your mind," he added when she started to complain about cherry-picked thoughts for a second time. "I know they've figured out a way to have some privacy."

She froze.

"What?" he asked, tucking her even closer.

"You'd do that?"

"Do what?"

"Put barriers between us." She frowned, shook her head. "That didn't come out right. I just mean, aren't men who are recently bonded all possessive and clingy and want to be as close as possible?"

It didn't make sense that he'd want anything between them.

"I want you to be happy," he said, shifting so she could see his face. "It's all I've *ever* wanted, but now? It's more than just an obscure *I hope she's happy.* Now, I want to feel that happiness here"—he tapped the spot on her chest above her heart —"and here"—fingers brushing her temple.

But wasn't that what everyone wanted? Any good person would want others to be happy and fulfilled. She just didn't get what that had to do with the bond. "I . . . don't understand," she whispered.

He laughed. "It's okay. Just know that, yes, I want to kiss and stroke and lick every inch of that sexy body of yours, but I also want you to be happy deep inside." Those chocolate eyes held his. "Because I don't think you've been happy deep inside, have you, Firefly?"

Suz glanced up at the sky, studied the blinking twinkles of the stars. "Tell me why you call me that."

"Avoiding my question?"

"Only so much as you've been avoiding mine."

He laughed, drawing a giggle out of her. "Okay," he said once they'd quieted. "We'll leave the questions."

A beat.

"For now," she said ominously.

He snorted then agreed, "For now."

"Muhaha."

"Come here."

She frowned, glanced over—or rather *up* at him. "I *am* here."

"Come closer."

"How?" she huffed. "I'm practically in your lap, Graham."

Hands on her hips, scooping her up, and plunking her down *into* his lap. "That's how," he said, and she knew he was smirking, even though he'd set her back against his chest and wrapped his arms around her so she couldn't escape.

Or maybe because he just wanted to hold her.

Because Suz couldn't deny it felt nice to be in the circle of his embrace, to feel his heat, smell his scent . . . sense the contentment through the bond.

Not hers, though she certainly was enjoying it.

Still, that contentment she felt was his, shining down like sunshine upon her skin, as though she had tilted her face up to the sky and was feeling the warm rays on her cheeks, her brow.

It was settled and comfortable and *nice*.

God, it had been so long since she'd just sat somewhere quietly, let alone with another person, a man, and one who was holding her so carefully, so gently—

Because of the bond, not necessarily that he wanted to spend time with her.

She released a short little breath. How could she forget the bond? It had to be helping with the intimacy, especially paired with the fact that she'd wanted him forever, but normally she wouldn't ever be able to relax with a man and not try to fill the silence.

But with Graham, she could sit here quietly and just be and enjoy the feel of his arms and—

"Shh," he whispered.

Her brows drew together. "I *am* being quiet."

His finger tapped lightly against her temple. "Not in here."

She sighed. "I can't just shut my brain off."

"Why not?"

Another sigh. "Because it's not that easy."

"Yes, it is."

She huffed. Again. What was it about this man that had her reduced to a sighing teenager? "You're just trying to piss me off."

"Maybe."

"You're a terror."

"Also, maybe."

"You—"

"But I'm also the terror who has the ability to make you turn off your brain."

"How—*oh!*"

He flipped her in his lap, spinning her so she straddled his waist, and then even as her surprised gasp passed her lips, his mouth was on hers.

And *God,* that was good.

The man radiated heat, and it was just chilly enough beneath the lightening sky that the warmth was welcome. Add in how his arm snaked around her waist, the gentle way his palm cupped her cheek, and she was lost. Though . . . her mind did quiet. Thoughts flew away as sensation took their place.

The sleek dart of his tongue.

The roughened pads of his fingers.

His chest, his legs, his—

Oh.

Now *that* was nice, she thought, winding her arms around his shoulders and settling deeper onto the hardened length of his erection. It would be even nicer if they were both naked, of course, especially since she now had personally experienced all that glorious hardness.

She especially liked it when he'd gripped her hips, tugged her forward on the edge of the desk, and plunged deep inside.

Graham pulled back, hot breath on her skin. "What did you just think?"

Her cheeks went hot, even as she pretended not to know what he was talking about. "Wh-what?"

A thumb brushing along her bottom lip, but he must have sensed she was lying through the bond—which was incredibly inconvenient—because he smirked, and she felt satisfaction trickle from his mind to hers.

"Was it something like this?" he murmured, tugging her closer as he kissed his way along her jaw.

"It was—*ah*—" Her breath caught as he positioned their hips, grinding against her.

That was glorious. Even through the layers of clothes.

But she wasn't going to admit it. Not even under pain of death.

"Not," she finished, even as pleasure slid over her skin, firing her nerves, making her thighs clench around him.

"Hmm." His tongue flicked out, tasting her, raising goose-flesh on her arms. "You sure?"

"Yup." Although even she could admit that it wasn't spoken steadily.

A pause.

Then she found herself off his lap, tucked against his side.

"I—" she said, fully aware that it wasn't the most intelligent of responses, even as she blinked at the speed with which he'd moved her. It probably should be annoying, as she'd never enjoyed people taking advantage of the fact that she was rather pocket-sized, but instead she found herself impressed by the way he moved. Graceful and rapid, barely jostling her in the process.

One second on top of him, the next at his side.

"You what?" he asked, resting his chin on her head.

She didn't know what he was talking about, nor even what she'd been thinking. She was a whole lot turned on and a whole lot tired, and suddenly she was starting to feel overwhelmed again.

Or maybe less overwhelmed and more sexually frustrated, or maybe she was—

Graham sighed. "I'm sensing a trend here."

Her brows drew together.

"Your brain." He lightly tapped her temple. "Tornado."

"That's not—"

"It is," he interrupted. "But that's one of the things I've always admired about you, Suz. You're smart and capable and even though sometimes you have the bedside manner of Nurse Ratched—"

"Hey!"

"You're still brilliant," he said. "And while I thought that staying away from you was the right thing, especially since I'm old and decrepit"—he smiled down at her, a smirk that demonstrated quite easily how he was leaps and bounds away from being old and/or decrepit—"but I've decided," he finished.

Just *I've decided.*

"What does that mean?" she asked.

A shrug. "I think the bond knew you needed me, even when neither of us recognized it."

The words were nice . . . kind of. Because she didn't like the idea of needing anyone, least of all this man who'd ignored her for so long—even *if* he were trying to chalk it up to doing right by her.

"Ah," she said.

"Suz?"

She felt his brain probing hers, a light tickle in the back of her mind, but she quickly side-stepped that presence, turning her focus to the trees.

Anything had to be better than the creeping feeling in her stomach.

The one that said she both couldn't be vulnerable, and also that Graham was just trying to make the best of a tricky situation—read: he didn't want to lose his magic, more so than he was interested in her. Both made her feel sick inside, and frankly, both made her feel pathetic. She should be taking a page from his book, lifting her chin and accepting her fate and finding a way forward.

But . . . she couldn't quite shrug it off.

Not when—

"Is Earth magic your specialty?" she blurted, desperate to turn away from her thoughts. She wasn't this uncertain, drifting creature. She was focused, and once she set her mind to something, she got her shit done.

He nodded but didn't give any indication about that tornado in her brain. Heaven help her, but it hadn't gone away. If anything, it was growing, spinning closer.

"It's always been really easy to grow things," he said. "What's yours?"

All Rengalla first learned their magic through the elements —each having an affinity for either fire, water, earth, or air. Earth specialists tended toward the greener aspects—florists, gardeners, landscape art, even though all Rengalla could couple their skills with secondary specialties, such as Suz's profession of healing.

"Water," she murmured. "I was forever overwatering the trees your kind were growing." She stifled a sigh, forced herself to keep her tone light. "You were probably cursing me every day of the week."

"I probably would have been," he said, "but I never had much patience for the landscape arts. As soon as I could, I went into defensive magic."

"Oh."

That was strange. Most Rengalla stayed in their vein of specialty for at least a little while.

Even her healing magic was derived from her affinity to water. She used the liquid between cells and inside cells, the various fluids in the body to focus in on the injuries she was healing.

"But it's not all growing plants," she said with a frown. "Those with earth magic built the Colony and they . . ." She trailed off, trying to recall something the earth crew did that wasn't related to plants or lumber or growing something. They tended the food the Rengalla ate, created the outdoor spaces, grew the trees they harvested for furniture. They even helped put together the electronic components—though oftentimes, the Rengalla just went out and purchased those. That was easier than creating a factory just so they could create a router.

But they *could* create a router.

With enough patience and magic, they absolutely could.

Same with laptops and computers, wiring and cell phones.

It was just . . . money wasn't a problem, and they had bigger problems than mass-producing the new iPhone whatever.

Plus, copyright infringement.

Plus, they were spoiled and—

There, she went off on another tangent.

"See?" he asked, trailing his fingers down her arm. "Plants and growing shit."

"But you grew this," she pointed out.

"That's true." A shrug. "Sometimes, the earth magic gets a little pent up and needs the exertion."

"That sounds terrible."

"I'll survive." He glanced down. "Want to tell me why we got on the topic of reviewing our magical prowess?"

"Ew," she muttered. "That sounds terrible."

"Suz," he said.

She ignored him. "I really like that tree," she said. "The one with the purple flowers. What's it called?"

"Jacaranda," he said then added without missing a beat. "What did I say?"

"Nothing." Her eyes stayed glued to those pretty purple flowers. "I just really like their coloring is all."

"Suz." A beat where she began counting those pretty purple flowers. Because it was much easier to count and then—*oh look*, there was a whole other branch with even more flowers to count. It was so much easier to not think about what was going on in her head instead of the ridiculous urge to want this bond to mean something when it clearly couldn't.

It was hours old, for fuck's sake.

And she was annoying even herself—okay, fine, so maybe she wasn't the most patient person in general—but this simpering *oh-no-he-might-not-like-her* shit was tiring.

She needed to get over it, and quickly.

"Hey," he whispered. "Firefly, it'll be—"

"Fine," she said, putting a little bit of space between them. She couldn't think clearly when he was so close. "Of course, it will be fine. It's just been a long day." That was the truth, and also her cue.

This was just too much, and she needed sleep and—

Repeat: it was just too much.

She'd reached her limit.

Standing, she allowed her gaze to flick to Graham's. But only for a second. He could already see in her mind, so he didn't need to see her expression and get further confirmation of how unhinged she was feeling.

"I'm going to bed," she announced.

He slowly came to his feet. "I'll walk you to your room."

"No."

It came out too sharp; she knew that.

But circling back to unhinged and terrified and feeling too fucking vulnerable.

His golden eyes held hers. "I'm going by myself," she said firmly.

A burst of frustration, of refusal in her brain, but he didn't voice those feelings aloud. Maybe he sensed how close she was to the edge, or perhaps he just had more self-control than she did. Either way, after a long moment, he just nodded and said, "I'll see you later today."

She crept back to the door, her fingers grasping the cold metal.

"Suz?" he said as she tugged it open.

Her feet skittered to a stop.

"Sweet dreams," he murmured.

Another nod. Her feet still frozen.

"Go on, Firefly." Still spoken so softly, so carefully.

With that, finally, she could move, could escape into the hall.

She sped through the winding, and thankfully empty, corridors, her footsteps clicking on the dark wooden floor, rapid movements that brought her quickly to her rooms.

Her palm on the door opened the lock and she burst inside, out of breath, sweat sheening her skin.

She stumbled into the shower, threw on pajamas.

And fate was with her.

For once that day, it was with her.

Exhaustion pulled her under almost the moment she snuggled under her blankets.

Almost.

Because just before she drifted off, she had the distinct thought—

Perhaps fate had actually been with her twice that day.

TEN

Graham

HE REMAINED in place long after the door closed behind Suz, realizing that this was going to be more complicated than he had anticipated.

Stupid to just now recognize that?

Certainly.

But several centuries on this planet didn't mean he was immune to that common male affliction. Snorting at one of his sister's favorite sayings, he lay back on the cushion and stared up at the sky. Pondering. Trying to untangle the tangle. Suz liked him. He could feel that with certainty. Suz wanted him. Also something he could feel with certainty. And Suz was terrified of him—though perhaps she was less terrified of him specifically and more terrified of what he and the bond represented.

Either way, he needed to take himself and his centuries and find some patience.

To tread carefully, win her over by inches.

God knew they had plenty of time on their hands.

The problem was that even though he knew that logically,

there was a pulse beating inside him, a constant *thrum-thrum* that had nothing to do with pumping blood through his body.

With a sigh, he stood, stashing the cushion and blanket away in the basket his sister had snuck into the space not long after he'd finished with the greenery.

How Amelia knew about it in the first place, he didn't know. It wasn't surprising because his sister was sneaky as fuck and one of the nosiest people he knew, but he'd kept his side project a secret on purpose.

Yet, she'd found out with enough accuracy to include a blanket, cushion, and basket exactly the right size.

All without a word.

But that was Amelia.

She was thoughtful and sweet, and this wasn't the first object that had appeared in his sphere.

New towels on the rack in his bathroom.

Warm cookies on his counter.

A new shirt in his closet—which, of course, had accompanied the throwing out of his favorite shirt. The latter had been beyond saving, at least according to his sister. But though he'd complained outrageously, he didn't mind so much. In truth, it was nice having Amelia do those things for him, especially since it had been ages since his mother had been capable of caring for anything except her own broken heart.

Ever since his father had been killed.

That day had been—

The memories threatened to slide out of that locked box in the back of his brain. The horror of that day. The pain. The blood. Trying desperately to do *something* when the reality was that it had been too late for anyone to do anything.

Then he was gone, and it had been Graham's job to pick up the pieces.

And God, Amelia had been just a baby then. Or at least a

child. With pigtails and skinned knees . . . and tear-filled blue eyes.

Always sad and sheened with tears.

Eventually, she'd come out of her shell and though there were a few years between her and Suz, they'd ended up becoming close during their secondary magic days. Amelia had been a bit behind, Suz a bit ahead, and they'd . . . met in the middle.

Which was what he needed to do, what he and Suz needed —to find that happy medium, even when his brain and body kept telling him to push, *push*, to find any way to get her to accept the bond, whether it be bullying, cajoling, or orgasming her into submission.

Patience.

Right.

But he didn't *want* to. Cue whining teenaged boy. He wanted her. *All* of her. Right. Now. He didn't want patience. He wanted inside her—and not just sexually. The bond was a tender thread in the back of his brain, a taunting, teasing presence that was pressing him to track her down in her rooms.

He wouldn't, of course.

He was more than a ball of hormones.

"Yeah, right," he muttered, remembering how beautiful she'd been spread out beneath him. How gorgeous and tempting and naked. Which wasn't really helping his ball problem.

Snorting, he spared one final look at his place and slipped out into the hall.

He placed his hand on the panel to lock the door then headed for his rooms.

Despite all the talk of nakedness and his balls, Graham knew he needed to regroup, needed to come up with a plan to convince Suz to open her heart—even with all that fear bundled inside her.

But first, he thought, pushing through the door to his own room, he needed to get some sleep.

He kicked off his shoes, stripped down, and crawled under the blankets.

A moment later, he let sleep pull him under.

He woke the moment the door to his quarters opened.

Sleep was a heavy weight on his eyes, threatening for a moment to drag his lids down, but he'd been a soldier too long to not be alert.

Still and silent in an instant.

Listening to footsteps come closer.

Then he heard a *clunk*, paired with a barely audible curse, and he relaxed immediately. Amelia.

Trying to sneak up on him.

Again.

He barely stifled the smile and slitted his eyes, letting them adjust to the dark, listening as she groped her way through the unlit hallway until he saw her emerge in his bedroom.

Then crept toward the bed.

He didn't move . . . well, his limbs anyway. Because he couldn't resist moving his lips.

"What are you doing?"

She shrieked, bumped into the corner of the wall, and fell over.

Probably, he should have helped her up.

But he couldn't—for two reasons. First, it was fucking hilarious to see her flailing on her back like an overturned turtle. Second, he was buck-ass naked and wasn't going to scar either of them like that.

Instead of getting out of bed, he stayed under the covers and laughed hysterically.

"You're so mean!" Amelia said, flopping for a few more seconds before she managed to right herself. "I was trying to surprise you!"

"No," he said. "You're trying to sneak up on me. Which"—he sat up, tucking the covers around his waist and arching a brow at her—"you can't even try to deny because I know you, Meely."

She flicked on the light, momentarily blinding them both.

Once he could see again, he saw that her nose was wrinkled.

"You know I hate that name," she grumbled.

"Tough," he said. "I played tea party with you for enough years to have carte blanche with nicknames."

"Hmph." Another grumble. "I should have made you play longer."

Laughter bubbled up in his chest. "Why are you really here, Meely?" he asked. "I know it isn't because you thought you could get the jump on me."

More nose wrinkling.

But he knew how to handle his sister.

Well, correction, he knew how to outwait her.

"What time is it?"

"Twelve-fifteen."

He'd gotten a few hours in, at least.

"How was work?"

A pause. A very long pause that told him he knew precisely the reason she was in his room. "Fine," she eventually said. "The kids were the kids, of course. But they're progressing really well."

His sister taught the third years and did a great job.

She had a natural knack with children, probably because she was practically a child herself.

Like Suz.

The bond throbbed in the back of his mind, an ever-present reminder of all that had changed, but at the same time, he knew that Suz wasn't like Amelia. In reality, she hadn't been for a long time.

"And Peter?" he asked, referring to the young pup who was currently dating his sister. "Is he still treating you well?"

"You mean since you asked me yesterday?" she said, leaning back against the wall and crossing her arms. "Yes, Peter is a gem and I love him and we're going to make copious amounts of little Rengalla."

"*What?*" He started to jump up, remembering in the nick of time that he was naked.

Meanwhile, it was Amelia's turn to laugh hysterically.

She bent at the waist, guffawing like a person twice her height, and when she straightened, her eyes, so much like his own, danced with amusement.

"You're not funny," he said—or well, he took his turn at grumbling.

"Except, I *am*." She smiled cherubically. "Also, I do love Peter, but I don't think we're ready for a herd of little children."

The idea of his sister having sex made him want to murder and shudder in equal parts, but he still felt obliged to point out, "You'd be great with a herd of children. Remember, I've watched you in action. You could even handle a flock."

She pretended to gag before coming over to sit on the edge of the bed. "The best part of my job is that I can send the kiddos home at the end of the day."

"True," he said distractedly. Because he wasn't thinking about his sister.

He was thinking about Suz and what she wanted.

And did she want kids?

Which was way beyond anything he should be thinking, but also . . . he was thinking it.

The only thing to do was to pretend that he hadn't had the thought.

Because his sister was sitting two feet away from him.

Pop.

Who smacked him across the chest. *Hard.*

"Ow," he muttered, rubbing the smarting spot. "What was that for?"

"You're not even going to *bring it up?*" she said—okay, screeched.

How had news about the bonding made the rounds already? That seemed impossible and yet, he knew his people and he knew who knew. And Mason was probably all about throwing him under the bus in order for someone else to be the focus for a little while. Still, he attempted to play it cool anyway. "I don't know what you're talking about."

A shake of her head. "Lies in a trash can."

"Well," he said, trying for distraction instead. "I guess I should get my naked ass out of bed."

"Naked?" More nose wrinkling.

"I do sleep that way."

"And that was a piece of information I could have lived without knowing." A beat. "Or seeing."

"And yet, you haven't left."

"I'm not leaving until you tell me everything."

"There's nothing to tell," he lied, peeling back the blanket and calling his sister's bluff.

She clamped her hands over her eyes but didn't move, the stubborn thing. "There's *everything* to tell!" Her voice dropped to a whispered. "People are saying that you've *bonded.*"

"Hmm." He stood, reached for a pair of sweats and tugged them on.

"Hmm?" she asked. "Just *hmm?*"

"Hmm."

A groan. "You're unbelievable, you know that?"

"I love you, too," he said, peeling her fingers off her eyes. "I'll stop by and see you and Mom on my dinner break, but I have a shift now. I need to get ready for that."

"*Graham,*" she groaned.

"*Meely,*" he countered, nudging her toward the door. "I'll see you later."

"But—"

He reached for the handle, pulled the heavy panel open. "*Later,* okay. I just—" Not that he remembered what he would have said.

Because Suz.

Whose pretty chocolate eyes warmed and whose mind suddenly flared brightly inside his, giving him a glimpse of her thoughts. Heat, desire, *need*, but also uncertainty and no little amount of fear. Which—the second part at least—felt like shit. The desire and need, yeah, that was something he could get behind. But the fear . . . that was a fucking knife to his gut.

He was just starting to know this woman as a woman and not a sister (even as much as that had been pretend), a healer, a casual friend, but he'd always known she wasn't someone who ran scared.

That was fact.

"Hey," she whispered, her chin coming up the smallest degree.

Fuck, but he liked that, *respected* that. He could feel that anxiety, and she was here anyway.

"Hey, Firefly," he said. "I was just coming to see you."

Her eyes flicked down then back up, and hell if he didn't feel that, feel as though her fingers were the ones doing the tracing. "You'd cause a riot," she murmured.

He grinned. "You saying you like my body?"

A huff, and God, he loved when she released that annoyed little puff of air. Her lips would form a perfect O and then she'd press them flat for a beat. "I'm *saying* that I came to see if you'd eaten since we were up so late, and I thought maybe we should go get something to eat."

"I have to work," he murmured, running the backs of his fingers across her cheek.

His mind tingled, filling with disappointment—from both him and her.

"Oh," she whispered. "That's okay. I just—"

"I missed you."

Her lips curved, she glanced at her watch. "It's been all of six hours. Most of which you were unconscious for."

Which was about five hours and fifty-nine minutes too long, his body and mind were screaming at him, but since he knew that was unreasonable and ridiculous, Graham was able to chuckle self-effacingly and tug on a lock of her hair. "Feels like longer."

She hitched a thumb over her shoulder. "I should go."

"Dinner?" he asked.

"Well, I—"

But it was to be another statement that he'd not know the end of.

Because that was the moment he remembered his sister was two feet behind him.

"I thought you were having dinner with us." Amelia shoved his shoulder, and he realized he was blocking the entire doorway with his body. "Move, you big lug," she muttered. "I want—" A grunt. "To see—" Another. "Who you are—" One more. "Talking to."

In front of him, Suz's lips parted, no sound coming out.

She retreated a step . . . at the same moment Amelia managed to shove him to the side enough to slip by him.

"You!" she gasped, sliding to a halt. "And Graham? What? I — *How*—?" She grabbed Suz's arm, practically jumping up and down. "Holy fucking shit!"

Horror flooded him.

From Suz.

"Amelia—"

"This is great," she said, bouncing on her toes. "You and I can be sisters, and we can plan a wedding—or well, a bonding ceremony. Tell me that I get to pick out a fancy dress and that we can convince the kitchens you *have* to do a cake tasting, like they do on all those reality TV shows. I watched one with Dee the other day and—*oh my God!* Daughtry! Does Daughtry know? Does Gabby? Does—"

Slowly, oh so slowly, he lifted his hand and cut off the flow of words.

"Go, Firefly," he whispered. "I'll see you soon."

White teeth pressing into a bottom lip. "*When?*"

But the question hadn't been out loud.

It was in his mind.

And it felt incredible, like the most intimate thing he'd ever heard or felt. It was as though Suz were in his mind, but not just her voice. Physical and audible and also strengthening the link connecting them. It was . . . right. The single most *right* thing he'd ever experienced in his life.

Another brush of his knuckles over her cheek. "*As soon as I can, Firefly.*"

That one word had sealed her fate.

He was keeping her.

ELEVEN

Suz

BONES.

They were such a pain in the ass.

Especially the little ones. The tiny groupings forming the ankle. The small bones of the metatarsals. They were so freaking finicky and frustrating to fix—shifting and floating out of place, the most infinitesimal fracture missed causing inordinate pain.

She hated it.

Give her blood and gore, sutures and stitches any day of the week.

Her magic slid over the bone, searching for any of those pesky cracks. The brown strands were microscopic in nature or would be to the naked eye, but she could "see" everything, or at least sense it.

Wrapping around, slipping in between cartilage and bone, looking and searching and—

She blinked, coming back into herself, her vision clearing as she met the eyes of her charge.

Bets was two hundred if she was a day, but she didn't look it. None of the Rengalla showed their age once they hit their mid-twenties. Well, Suz supposed that wasn't entirely true. The Rengalla aged, just incredibly slowly, those twenties turning to thirties over many decades.

But of all the ages to make her way slowly through, Suz couldn't complain.

"What's the verdict, Doc?"

"The verdict is that you'd done a number on your ankle," she said, shifting away and moving to the computer to log the injury, thankful that she'd made the switch to digital records as soon as technology had allowed. Several centuries of broken ankles, glued chins, vaccinations, allergies, and flu were more than her brain could categorize for one patient, let alone an entire Colony's worth. "But the verdict is," she added before Bets could get too worried. "I've fixed the breaks and the torn cartilage—"

Paper crinkled before she could finish the rest of her statement.

Bets wasn't much for hospitals, and even though the infirmary was only a tiny one, she still never made an appearance unless she absolutely had to.

The inverse was also true.

She'd make a break for it at the soonest possible moment.

"Freeze," she ordered before Bets's foot could hit the floor. "I need to get you crutches," she said. "And you'll *use* them. Otherwise, I'll move to a wheelchair. *And*"—she spoke over Bets's protests—"if you don't abide the wheelchair, that'll be bed rest."

"Suz," she whined.

"I mean it," Suz said, not falling for the whine.

"But you fixed the break." Still whining.

And still not falling for that whine. "Yes, but it'll be fragile for the next few weeks," she pointed out. "So, that means no weight bearing for the first week and then light use only for the next two."

"But—"

She tapped a few final keys and stood, moved to the door.

"Where are you going?"

"To get a wheelchair."

"You wouldn't—"

Suz glanced back, lifted a brow.

Silence. For a long moment. Before Bets's brightly painted fire-engine red lips pressed together. Then a heavy sigh, paired with a begrudging, "I'll take the crutches."

"Wise choice," Suz said, smothering a smile as she went to the cabinet and retrieved a pair. It only took a few moments to get them adjusted and before long, Bets was high tailing it down the hallway and out the front door, calling over her shoulder, "Don't think that just because I didn't mention that fancy magic covering you that I didn't notice!"

Suz groaned. "Fucking hell." Why had the bond decided to coat her in the combined magic? Why had it decided to make her a walking announcement that she belonged to Graham?

The only positive was that he was marked, too, so it wasn't some super macho *this is my woman, hands off* bullshit.

Or at least if it were, it went both ways.

But double the magical coating meant double the people in the Colony would find out about the bond, and then those people would tell other people, and pretty soon everyone on the planet would know and—

Would that really be such a bad thing?

Her stomach still churned at the thought of having a man—or any person—inside her brain, hearing everything that went through her mind.

He would find her lacking. It was inevitable.

God knew that wouldn't be anything new.

Plenty of people had found her deficient, incapable of being what they needed, left wanting after she'd given all she could give.

Except, she'd gone to see him this morning, and he hadn't seemed disappointed or left wanting or otherwise. In fact, he'd been thrilled that she was there, his happiness at seeing her outside his door a warm burst of sunshine in her mind.

And for the woman who'd warred with herself the entire way to his room—chickening out fighting the need to be herself, to be strong, powerful, and confident, fear warring with taking what she needed—it had meant so much. Especially, after she'd spent the walk nearly turning back more than a handful of times, having to force her hand to the door (not even getting around to knocking).

"Hey—" Gabby appeared in the doorway, crossing the room and helping Suz tear the paper covering off the bed, dragging down a fresh swathe. "Do you need a break before you clear the waiting room?"

Suz paused. "What's out there?" Maybe *Who's out there?* would have been a more prudent question, but she stood by her inquiry. If they had an influx of patients, she'd need to triage.

"Just three yearly physicals out front," Gabby told her. "But the rooms are full."

Shit.

"With what?" she asked.

"With what appears to be bruised ribs in room one, but I'm not skilled enough to know for sure," Gabby said and began ticking off on her fingers. "Split chin in room two. The broken ankle in here. And then what appears to be a case of Man Flu, a pregnancy, a sprained wrist, a fever, and an earache in rooms four through eight."

"Full moon or something?" Suz muttered. There hadn't

been any other patients when she began to work on Bets's ankle, but it always seemed like the celestial changes made it so there was a parade of Rengalla through her front door.

Sometimes that was fun.

Today, when she was exhausted from the previous day's events, not so much.

But this was her job, her calling. Her *soul*.

Gabby smiled. "Unfortunately, my skills don't extend to knowing the moon phases."

"So disappointing."

A snort. "I'll borrow a book from the library. Be prepared for next time."

Suz laughed then got down to business. "The fever is first," she said, rolling her shoulders. "Then the split chin, followed by the earache. Then the rest of 'em. Can you speak to the others and make sure they're okay with waiting?"

"Of course."

"Then if you're up to it, do you feel comfortable doing the physicals? I can pop in to speak with them, but if you can do measurements and vitals, that would help us speed through."

"Should I call in Doreen?" Dor was another healer and although mostly retired, she did spell them when the infirmary got packed, especially since Gabby was still learning how to use her magic and healing took an exceptional toll.

"No," Suz said. "She's off on a picnic with her grandkids today. Can you find out if Cody isn't bogged down with LexTal duties, see if he can lend an hour or two?"

"Sure." A beat. "Fever is in room seven."

"Got it."

Gabby left with a little wave.

"Okay," she murmured to herself, pausing for a moment to fix her ponytail and to take a breath.

Then she got to work.

The fever turned out to just be a childhood bug, but since Jess's baby was little and Jess was a new mom, Suz took a few extra minutes and used her magic to give the infant a thorough scan.

"Sophia's fine," Suz said once it was complete. "Her immune system is fighting hard."

"But she's so hot," Jess said, brushing her hand over Sophia's fawn-colored hair.

"Yes, honey. That's her body working to make her feel better." Suz moved to the cabinets and pulled out a thermometer. "This," she said, "is the most accurate thermometer on the market." It wasn't, but Jess didn't know that. "Your job is to take her temperature once an hour, and if it goes over one hundred and one, you call me. Can you do that?"

"I—" Jess's bottom lip trembled for a moment before they pressed together. Then she nodded. "Yes."

"Good." Suz moved to the sink and washed her hands then input what she needed into the computer as she gave a few more instructions about continuing to nurse so little Sophia would stay hydrated. "Okay, honey?"

"Okay," Jess whispered.

"Now, go home and get some rest. I'm calling Colleen"— Jess's partner—"to have her come home as well."

"But she's working, and she has a big project going. I don't want to mess—"

"This is more important." Suz pushed away the keyboard and turned back to Jess. "And you know she'll think exactly the same as I do."

Jess's blue eyes were damp. "It's supposed to be my turn to handle things." That bottom lip trembled again. "I'm supposed to be able to handle this. What good am I if I can't take care of—"

"She's got a cold, honey. That's not anybody's fault."

"But—"

"It's not," she said firmly enough to make Jess stand up straighter. "Now, go home. Try to get some rest, and let me know if anything changes, okay?"

"Okay."

With that, and relieved that Jess had been too upset to notice that Suz was covered in Bond Magic, she slipped out of room seven, moving down to room two, but before she made it, she heard Cody's voice through the closed door, taking care of the split chin inside. Pausing a moment to pop her head in long enough to make sure he had things well in hand, she continued on with clearing the rest of the backlog.

The earache was an easy fix, just needing a quick blip of magic in order to clear the impacted wax. Then she moved on to the ribs, while Cody took care of the wrist. Which left the pregnancy and the Man Cold.

She crossed paths with the muscled mass of green-eyed prettiness known as Cody in the hallway, who groaned when she told him the cases that were left.

"Men are the biggest babies," he muttered, taking a step toward room four.

"Are you so severe upon your own sex?"

Another groan. "Don't tell me," he grumbled. "You've watched that movie with Dee again."

"What movie?"

"*Pride and Prejudice.*"

So, maybe she had. Maybe she was quoting it. Although it hadn't been with Dee. She'd been by herself, unable to sleep a few nights before, and she'd watched it twice, polishing off a bottle of wine, along with two bags of popcorn. She'd swooned over the rain scene, sighed at the grazed hands, and felt ridiculously jealous at the *I love, I love, I love you.*

But she wasn't going to admit that to the man in front of her.

"I don't know what you're talking about."

"Uh-huh, sure you don't," he said. "And I'll just pretend that I don't see that Bond Magic coating your skin."

"I *still* don't know what you're talking about."

"Liar." He tugged the end of her ponytail, then rolled his eyes when a groan echoed out into the hallway. A male groan. That was paired with copious amounts of sighing. "I'll deal with the Man Cold. You do the pregnancy check-up. Then you, me, and Gabby will blitz through those physicals before I buy you dinner."

"You mean bring me free food from the cafeteria."

"Well, obviously."

She bit back a grin. "It's a deal. Though, if you need to go, I can handle the rest. You've already saved the day."

"That's what we LexTals do," he said, walking backward toward room four and the Man Cold. "We're heroes."

"And you're so modest, too."

He grinned, saluted, then slipped into the room, leaving her to make her way to the pregnancy.

That was a fun appointment, and she got to share with the expectant parents that they were having a little boy, who was growing quite well and would be stealing their sleep in the very near future.

But the promised food from Cody didn't materialize.

He was pulled away, needed at some self-defense training for the youngest soldiers. She couldn't complain, wouldn't ever complain. As a LexTal, his duties were first and foremost to the defense of the Colony, and that included making sure their soldiers could protect themselves.

She powered through the physicals, ignoring the comments on the magic glittering over her skin and still feeling like a walking advertisement. But even so, she cleared the remaining people who'd trickled into the waiting room throughout the day, and only finally when her feet were screaming, her shoulders absolutely aching with pain, did she close the door and turn off the lights.

Emergencies would be the only thing to pull her from the mound of paperwork in her office.

Rolling her neck, she made her way back down the hall, hoping that for a change, there wouldn't be any late-night calls.

She wanted to see Graham.

She'd felt him in the back of her brain all day, filling her with warmth, and for once, she didn't want her job interfering with her private life.

She wanted a private life.

No, she wanted Graham.

Graham, who'd looked so sexy that morning. Graham, who'd—

"Shit!" She straightened. Graham, who'd come by earlier and suggested they'd meet at seven to eat and talk and—

Her eyes flew to the clock.

Seven-forty-nine.

Fuck.

She grabbed a hoodie from the hook just inside her office, yanked it on, and hustled toward the door.

Maybe she could catch up with him.

Maybe she could—

She stumbled into the hall.

Stumbled because the moment she turned the handle, the door flew open, and she tripped, falling over . . .

Graham.

"Hi, Firefly," he murmured.

His mind in hers flared bright, as though they'd been on not quite the right frequency all day. And now suddenly with him in front of her, his hands on her shoulders, steadying her, they were fully in tune.

He was there and . . . it was fucking perfect.

"Hi," she whispered, soaking up the gloriousness of being next to him, of the bond in her mind, of his pretty freaking face—

His lips quirked, a sliver of amusement skating through her mind.

"No cherry-picking my thoughts, Crumbles," she muttered.

One brown brow lifted. "Crumbles?"

"Graham isn't an easy name to come up with a nickname." A shrug. "All I could think was cracker. But I can't exactly call you that, can I?"

He snorted. "Not the most romantic of statements, that's for sure."

"So, Crumbles." She shrugged.

His fingers trailed down her arm, laced with hers. "Not sure that's the most romantic of statements either."

"Want to tell me what Firefly means?" she asked, her body drifting closer. "Because that might convince me to keep pondering and to come up with something better." She tapped her chin. "Like Pookey Bear."

There was a flicker in her mind . . . something almost like embarrassment, but it was gone so quickly that she barely had time to process it. "I'll stick with Crumbles."

"I rather like Pookey Bear."

He tsked. "Behave."

Except, his hands had wrapped around her hips and were drawing her closer. Then closer still. Until she was pressed against his chest, all of those glorious muscles surrounding her.

"I think I like it when I don't behave."

"Yeah?" A bolt of wickedness sliding across their link. "Why's that?"

"It gets me closer to you."

Slow and sexy, that smile filled his face, made his eyes

dance, brought him even closer—or at least, it brought his lips closer.

His body was already plastered against hers.

She curled her fingers into his shirt, clutching him to her. "We can go back inside and—"

Her stomach growled.

And in a millisecond, his mind changed. The waves of heat pulsing off his mind, sliding through hers, skating down her spine disappeared. In its place was frustration. No. *Fury.*

"When was the last time you ate?" he growled, stepping back and cupping her cheeks.

Since she was still reeling from the loss of contact, all she could say was, "What?"

"You're starving," he snapped. "I can feel it pulsing through your mind. Did you eat at all today?"

"I—"

She stopped. One, because her stomach growled again, and two . . . well, because she couldn't remember the last time she'd eaten.

"Suz."

She jumped. "I—"

His eyes narrowed, and he was still scowling at her.

Yanking her head free, she did some glaring of her own. "Stop growling at me. The day was insane, and I—*oh!*"

Her words were cut off by him scooping her into his arms and carrying her down the hall.

"What are you doing?" she hissed.

"I'm feeding you."

"Um, no, you're *carrying* me," she said. "Down the hall. Where anyone and everyone can see."

"And?"

Sighing, she smacked him on the chest. "*And* I can walk. I have two feet and two legs, and if you just let me down I can—"

"Hush."

Not spoken aloud.

Instead, it was in her mind.

And her initial reaction—pleasure at feeling him there—meant that she didn't immediately struggle for him to put her down. Well, that and the fact that it felt really fucking good to be held by him.

"Put me down," she muttered when she remembered herself. "Now."

"I kind of like you here."

"You're going to *kind of like* my foot up your ass unless you put me down."

"Yeah?" he asked, eyes dancing, amusement lacing his tone *and* mind. "You think you can take me on?"

"I *know* I can."

A thumb brushing the inside of her arm, stroking across her bicep. "With these puny things?"

"Hey! They're not puny."

Just because they weren't the tree trunks that were holding her didn't mean she wasn't strong. She lifted patients. She worked until most other Rengalla would pass out.

"No," he said. "They're perfect." A beat, his voice in her mind. *"Just like the rest of you."*

She laughed. *"You can't possibly mean that."*

"I mean it," he whispered. *"Perfect for me."*

"You can't possibly mean *that*. It's been like one day and—"

"Don't." He skidded to a stop, rubbed his nose to hers. "Don't minimize what this is between us. Maybe it's new. Maybe it's just the potential of something. But I know"—he tapped her chest, just above her heart—"I know in *here* that if we play this right, if we both go for it, that this will be the best thing we can ever do for each other."

Her pulse was pounding like heavy feet on the pavement. *Thunk-thunk. Thunk-thunk. Thunk-thunk.*

The words that emerged weren't the ones she'd wanted to say.

They were still the most important ones she *could* have said.

"I'm not an easy person to love."

Silence.

Then, "I never asked for easy."

Swallowing hard, she opened her mouth, her mind curiously blank as she scrambled for anything to say that would encompass how strongly that small sentence had affected her.

Instead of asking her to explain her sudden silence, he kissed her.

Or perhaps, instead of forcing herself to find the words, *she* kissed *him*.

TWELVE

Graham

THE KISS she laid on him scorched him from his head to his socks, tempted him to turn around and carry her right back into the infirmary for a repeat of the night before.

Except . . . she was hungry.

And it was his job to care for her.

He tore his lips away, rested his forehead against hers, breath coming in rapid gusts, even as he tried to find some thread of control. Which wasn't fucking easy, not with his cock throbbing and her desire blazing across the bond.

Luckily, the fates seemed to be on his side.

At least marginally.

Her stomach growled again, even louder, and he found that the need to protect and care for Suz was stronger than his aching erection. Or maybe just his blue balls. Because he didn't think his cock was going to be changing its state anytime in the near future.

He set her on her feet.

Her eyes flashed to him. "Wh—"

"Food," he grunted, taking her hand.

"I'm not hungry for food," she said, sidling up to him. "I think . . . I *know* I want something else."

"You're going to wither away to nothing."

She patted her waist. "I'm certainly not going to wither away, not with these hips."

Considering he'd had his hands spanning them the night before, caressing those lush curves, he took exception to her disparaging one of his favorite body parts. But she was hungry, and he needed to make sure she was fed and rested and didn't want for anything. Because she was good and smart and *his,* and she shouldn't want for anything and—

"Now you've got the spinning tornado of thoughts," she murmured, tapping his temple. "That's usually my job."

"Food," he grunted, tugging her forward.

"I'm not hungry."

"Liar."

She chuckled, and it slid over his skin like warm honey. "Okay, I *am* hungry," she muttered. "Just not for food."

Silence.

Then they both burst out laughing.

Her head dropped to his shoulder. "It's the bond's fault."

"That you want me?"

She scowled up at him. "No. That I'm willing to choose sex over food."

He grinned.

"And it's not because you're so good." Another scowl, this time paired with her smacking him lightly on the chest. "So, don't get a big head about it." Another smack when he snorted. "It's just . . . it had just been a while, okay?"

"I'm not saying a word."

"You learn fast."

"Just because I've been single for a long time doesn't mean

I've never had a girlfriend," he said. "I know when to shut my mouth."

"But *do* you?"

He grinned. "Occasionally."

She snorted. "So, no sex?"

"Food, Firefly."

A huff.

"Then sex."

"Yeah?"

"But only if you're good."

Her brows lifted, her lips curved into a smirk. "How will I be good? Do I need to clean my plate?"

"That." He grinned down at her. "And other things."

"Hmm. *What* other things?"

Graham slowed to a stop and leaned closer, shifting until her chest was pressed to his, those soft breasts against him the best feeling ever. "You need . . ." His tongue flicked out, grazed her earlobe. "To do the dishes, too."

She'd melted at the touch of his tongue. His words made her stiffen, pull away. "You're not funny."

"Ah, but I am." A beat. "A little bit, anyway."

Her sigh was both mental and audible, and it made his grin grow even wider. "Funny *looking*," she muttered.

"Come on, Firefly," he said, taking her hand again. "Let's fill your belly."

The thread of mischief flitted through his mind, even before he heard her speak the words.

"Then you'll fill something else?"

He tripped.

She cackled.

And his heart was full.

Even as his stomach was empty.

"Come on, Trouble," he said, taking her hand and leading her down the hall.

The cafeteria had been his first mistake.

Because there were several dozen pairs of eyes on them. Nosy, prying eyes, glancing from him to Suz, to their interlaced hands, the magic covering their exposed skin.

And the smiles—the *knowing* smiles, actually—were real.

So was the glare Suz was tossing in his direction.

"They were bound to find out sooner or later, Firefly," he murmured.

"Later," she grumbled. "I really would have preferred for it to be later."

He nudged her to the counter, toward the delicious smells wafting their way. "Smells like Lex made homemade pizza. Your favorite."

Wide brown eyes flying to his. "How?" she whispered.

"Did I know?" he asked then leaned close and said softly, "I have spies everywhere."

She rolled her eyes, but he caught the thread of pleasure in her mind. "How can you possibly have spies everywhere when this is the first time the gossip train has seen us together?"

"Why don't we chalk it up to me being motivated to understand the woman I'm linked permanently to?"

In truth, he'd known that Suz's favorite meal was Lex's homemade BBQ chicken pizza well before today, but this was a happy coincidence he was more than willing to take advantage of, especially as he'd heard her and Amelia waxing poetic about the perfect ratio of sauce to cheese to crust more than a few times.

"Hmm."

"Don't believe me?" he asked, picking up a plate and scooping three large pieces onto it. Then grabbing another and repeating the process for himself.

"Hungry?"

He picked up the plates and nudged her forward. "This is for both of us."

"You expect me to eat three slices?"

"Yes." He put a scoop of fruit and some salad on both of the plates. "You haven't eaten all day."

"And I'm not gargantuan like you," she said. "I don't need that much food."

"I resent that comment," he said, attempting light, but he didn't mind the teasing and knew she could feel that. He liked that she could tease him. What he *didn't* like was Suz mistreating herself. So for good measure, he shoved a couple of breadsticks on their plates. "Come on," he said, nodding at an open table that was somewhat away from the rest of the gossips.

Not that it would stop them from being interrupted.

But at least they might be granted a few minutes of privacy while they ate.

Or not.

Because the moment he'd gotten Suz's cute little butt in a chair, Morgan strolled over. "Don't tell me that you're going to break my heart," he said, deliberately shoving between Suz and Graham.

Graham slid himself and the plates back a couple of inches, namely because he didn't want Morgan's ass on his pizza.

Suz giggled.

Giggled.

Now, it was his turn to scowl. She didn't giggle for him. Granted, they'd barely spent any time together, but she was supposed to be giggling for him, and only him.

No. Not *only* him.

He wasn't the type of man or boyfriend or bondmate to be jealous or to go all caveman *you-mine-and-only-mine.* But he was feeling exceptionally *you-mine-and-only-mine,* especially with Morgan so close. Everyone always said that the LexTal was the prettiest of his brothers with his "dreamy hazel eyes." Plus, Morgan was always making everyone laugh, including Suz and her giggles, and—

A pulse down their mental link, Suz's voice in his mind. *"I prefer golden eyes, myself."*

He glanced up from where he'd been scowling at his pizza, saw that she had leaned around Morgan in order to meet his eyes. *"You do?"* he asked.

A shrug, her gaze going heavy-lidded. *"Plus, the rest of the package isn't too bad either."*

His lips curved. *"It isn't?"*

"I like you, Graham. In case you hadn't noticed me trying to jump your bones in the hall."

"Well, I just figured it was my pure sexual magnitude that had struck you dumb."

"Dumb?"

Shit. *"It's just an expression."*

"Sure, it is."

Fuck. She'd been trying to make him feel better for being a jealous, insecure asswipe, and now he'd gone and insulted her. *"Firefly, I—"*

"I'm teasing." Her brow lifted. *"Something you'd normally register. Are you okay?"*

Okay?

Hell no, he wasn't okay. He was a fucking mess and—

"Crumbles?"

Not the nickname. *"Suz—"*

Morgan groaned.

They both looked at him, blinking, and Graham had the

sudden feeling of emerging from a soundproof room—noise blaring to full volume, the rest of the world abruptly intruding.

"Don't tell me you have the bond speak thing down *already?*" Morgan said on a sigh, looking from Suz to Graham.

"The what?" Suz asked.

"You know what I mean," Morgan said, reaching for a piece of pizza before Graham smacked his hand away. "The telepathy along the bond. Except you two are such overachievers you didn't even realize you're doing it already, did you?" He extended a hand toward their plates, Suz's this time. "What has it been, all of two days since you bonded?"

"One," Graham growled, smacked the hand a second time. "Now, go away."

"I'm hungry," Morgan whined.

"No, you're nosy," Suz said.

"That's not true," Morgan protested. "I'm nosy *and* hungry, and your bondmate there took the last slices of BBQ pizza."

Graham shrugged, clenching his fingers into his thighs, trying to resist the urge to throttle the other man. Yes, he'd once considered Morgan a friend, but the man was fucking annoying —and altogether too close to *his* woman. "I'm sure Lex has another in the oven."

"But it's not ready now."

"Here," Suz said on a sigh, picking up one of her slices and holding it out. "Take mine and go away."

Morgan clamped a hand to his heart. "You wound me."

But the fucker started to grab the pizza.

"You touch my mate's food, and I will cut you in half."

Graham had said the statement so conversationally that at first, he didn't think Morgan processed it. Then the other man froze, turning to look at him with raised brows. "She offered it."

"She's hungry and hasn't eaten all day. Go get your own food."

"Ugh," Morgan muttered, pushing off the edge of the table. "And here I thought you were going to be the sensible one who didn't get his brain muddled by your magic."

Graham just narrowed his eyes.

Morgan lifted his hands and walked away.

Thankfully, that left them blessedly alone.

"I should have just bribed Lex to give me a full pizza to go," he said sourly, picking up his first slice.

"But at least we're overachievers?"

"We're something," he muttered.

"Why are you grumpy?"

"Morgan is a pain in my ass."

"Morgan is a pain in *everyone's* ass." She slid her chair a little closer. "You okay?"

"I'd be better if you ate."

"I've waited all day. I can wait a little longer." She touched his arm. "What's up?"

What was up was his brain screaming at him that he wasn't taking care of her properly, that she was hungry and had been delayed by work, by Morgan, and now by him and his feelings.

"Eat," he ordered.

Suz crossed her arms, eyes flashing. "Is that an order?"

He spared one moment for *shit, she's going to be really pissed because that* was *an order* before he rocked forward, held his piece up to her mouth, and admitted, "Yes, it was a fucking order. You need someone to take care of you, since you're doing such a piss-poor job."

Her lips pressed flat.

Fuuuck.

Normally, he was better at communicating than this.

Normally, he didn't have his emotions tornadoing inside his head, sending everything he thought he knew scattering this way and that. Sucking in a breath, he scrubbed his free hand over his face. "Look, Firefly," he said, trying to keep a hold of his temper, knowing it was the bond screwing with him, taking what were normally strong protective instincts and ramping them to an intensity that threatened to make him lose control. Then add in a dash of jealousy and insecurity just to round things out and make it fun for everyone. "I'm struggling here."

Her face went blank, but he felt the pulse. "I told you I wasn't easy," she whispered, the tone carefully even, but it did absolutely nothing to hide the pain in her words, her mind.

"And I told you, I didn't ask for easy," he said, holding her gaze. "It's not you that I'm struggling with. I'm trying to reconcile what the bond is making me feel and to not act like a complete caveman."

She nibbled on the corner of her mouth. "What does *that* mean?"

"It means," he said, leaning very close, "that if you looked into my mind at this moment, you would see that I'm one hairsbreadth away from tossing you over my shoulder and carrying you off to my rooms where I force-feed you enough calories to fuel your body then tie you to the bed and make certain you sleep for eight full hours."

Her lips formed an O.

Then he felt the tentative presence in his mind, hers lightly probing his, exploring the walls he'd thrown up to stop himself from acting like a Neanderthal.

He let her in.

He *had* to.

She was his mate, his other half. He would never be able to keep her at a distance.

But the moment he dropped those walls, the moment she was fully inside his consciousness, she went still and sucked in a breath.

"Suz?" He threw the walls back up, reached for her hand. "Are you okay?"

"That's what you're feeling?" she asked, shifting so her palm met his, so their fingers wound together. "Graham, that's . . ."

He slapped on a smile.

"A lot."

"I'm fine."

"You're not fine," she whispered into his mind, but she picked up a slice and started eating, assuaging at least one small fire inside him. *"How are you coping with all of it?"*

He grabbed his own pizza. *"I've got experience coping with a lot of things. I can handle this."*

"How can I make it better?" she asked after she'd chewed and swallowed.

"It'll get better on its own," he said. "I talked to Mason some earlier. He says it's always worse for the guy, especially right in the beginning. Once . . . things are a bit more established, it'll improve."

"You think?"

"I *know.*" He smoothed back a piece of her hair. "It's already better just being here with you."

"Yeah?"

He nodded.

"Okay."

Fingers on her cheek, her jaw, soaking in the silken feel of her skin, holding it tight and allowing it to center him. "It would also help if you kept eating that freaking pizza you love so much," he said once he felt more in control, tone firmly in the realm of soft.

She smiled and took a giant bite.

Something inside him relaxed.

Well, not something so much as those protective urges, the worst of that tornado. Suz was here and she was letting him be close to her, allowing him to take care of her. That made it all okay.

That would make everything okay.

"Want to tell me about your day?" he asked.

She nudged his plate toward him. "Only if you eat, too."

He chuckled. "*I* ate today."

"Well, that gargantuan body of yours doesn't just run on insults and stubbornness."

"You lie." But not about to argue further, he picked up his own slice, and suddenly ravenous, he began gobbling it down.

Because she was also taking care of him.

That's what mates did.

THIRTEEN

Suz

SHE'D TRIED to get Graham to come in the night before, but instead he'd given her a kiss that made her head spin and her fellow Rengalla—who suspiciously had something to do in the corridor outside her room right at that precise moment—whoop and catcall.

But he'd left her on the threshold, heart pounding, legs like Jell-O, and with a wicked smile that filled her with . . .

Some deep emotion she wasn't looking at too closely.

Not when she worried her crush from all those years would overshadow her good sense.

Except, good sense was hard to hold on to in the face of a man like Graham. Especially, she realized as she flicked on the light in her office and saw the basket on top of her desk, when he unleashed his special brand of caring.

Biting her lip, she stepped toward the innocuous white hamper, peeked inside.

And her heart melted.

The deep emotion blooming.

The man was *good*.

A glass of orange juice, still cold based on the condensation on the outside of the cup, sat on one side of the basket. The inside of the wicker container was lined with a jaunty red-and-white-checkered napkin, and in the center of it was . . .

A pair of glazed donuts.

They smelled fucking incredible.

"You found them?"

Graham's voice in her head didn't come as a surprise, not when his presence had been there, all warm and sunshine-like, from the moment she'd woken up. But it still made her nerves stand on edge, every cell in her body focused on him.

"I did," she thought. *"Thank you. I won't be able to fit into my jeans if you keep this up."*

She felt his smile. *"I'll buy you bigger ones."*

Suz giggled, feeling his mind blaze brighter inside hers, his pleasure fueling hers until she knew she was probably grinning like an idiot. Still, she focused enough to send, *"Thank you, Crumbles."*

"I'm still not sure on that nickname."

"Not sure enough to tell me what Firefly means?"

A beat. *"Enjoy your breakfast."*

"Stubborn."

"To take your words, it fuels me." She sniffed, knew he could feel it, because his humor slid into her mind. *"I also put an apple in there, so you could at least pretend to be healthy."*

Her heart skipped a beat as her eyes flicked to the shiny red fruit. She'd been too excited about the donuts to see the attempt at forming a balanced meal.

"With the orange juice, it's practically a salad."

"Exactly." A beat. *"Can I see you later?"*

"I think after the pizza and donuts, the question is, will you be able to keep me away?"

"My evil plan has worked," he thought. *"I never expected it to take junk food."*

"Well, it was a damned good start."

"What do you want for lunch?"

Her cheeks hurt from smiling. *"Have your spies failed you?"*

"Never."

"Well," she thought. *"I'll let you make your best guess."*

"Mean."

"You'll survive."

His mental voice was light. *"Still mean."*

"I think you'll still survive."

He laughed, and the way it flittered across the bond made her veins feel as though they were filled with helium. *"I'd better let you eat before that waiting room of yours gets full."*

No doubt that would happen before too long.

"Graham?" she thought when she felt his mind retreating.

"Yeah, Firefly?"

"Thanks."

A mental kiss paired with a firm, *"Eat,"* and Suz knew she was in trouble. Deep feelings were getting even deeper.

And she'd been under the influence of Graham for all of two days.

But even as the fear of being sucked under, of losing herself, of the likelihood that he would look too deeply and find her wanting, bloomed, Suz knew she wasn't going to step back.

She had too much to lose.

Still, as she ate the donuts, drank the orange juice, chomped on the apple, feeling his mind grow fainter, she wondered if it was her magic she was worried about losing or her heart.

Wondered?

Okay, no. She already knew which of those two it was.

LUNCH, it turned out, wasn't to be.

The day had actually begun quietly, just her regular roster of appointments with no emergencies or urgent cases. No blood or broken bones or even fevers. It was all checkups and physical therapy.

In fact, she was so damned bored by the time Graham showed up with a tray of food that she could have kissed him right there in the waiting room.

Fine.

She *did* kiss him and pretended not to hear the catcalls.

Then she tugged him down the hall to her office, shutting the door behind him, and . . . then *he* kissed her.

There weren't any catcalls, but she still completely forgot about the food.

Which was saying something because she'd spotted what was on that tray, and it was a very rare thing for her to forget about homemade fettuccine with Lex's tomato cream sauce.

The chef had to be bribed in the best of terms to make it — since Lex took homemade things to the extreme. He ground his own flour, made his own noodles, grew then blanched, peeled, and cooked the tomatoes for the sauce. Hell, he'd probably milk the cows if he hadn't been warring with the head of the very capable team who took care of the Rengalla's livestock.

Which was a story for another day.

The point was that the man was scrupulous and detail-orientated, and his meals were a treat, especially his pasta recipes. He'd learned them in Tuscany more than a century before, then had spent decades perfecting them.

And she benefited.

Except when she didn't get to eat the results.

The first delay wasn't bad because being held by Graham, his hands and mouth working in tandem, was a positive deferral.

She'd take cold pasta paired with those weak knees and swollen lips any day of the week.

The second delay was more problematic.

Because it pulled her away from both her pasta *and* Graham's glorious mouth.

She didn't hear the knocking at first, not when she was in his arms and under the influence of all that Graham-ness. But pretty soon, the knocking grew louder and was accompanied by Gabby's concerned voice.

Graham released her, turned for the door, and opened it.

Gabby was pale, her eyes wide and darkened with concern.

In one moment, desire was on the back burner. Suz moved toward her assistant. "What is it?"

"I—um." A sharp shake of her head. "An emergency in quadrant three. Dante says that you need to be out there immediately."

"Okay, can you call Dor in to handle anything that comes up?"

A nod.

"I'll just grab my bag—"

"I've got it," Graham said. "Let's go."

Without another word, they sprinted down the hall, out of the infirmary, and hauled ass out of the building. The area surrounding the living and recreational quarters of the Colony was vast and green, filled with trees and trails and wilderness. Quadrant three was the most distant of the trio immediately surrounding the buildings, within the shield that protected them, and more open fields than forest.

"Were you able to telepath anyone?" she asked as they ran. "Find out the details of the patient?"

It was always easier to know going in, easier to prepare herself if something—

Graham's hand found hers, squeezing lightly.

"Someone's critical. Unconscious. Cody's there and trying to heal, but—" He paused, the only noise their feet on the ground as they ran, the bag *thunking* against Graham's back with each step.

"But what?"

"It's not working."

Her heart sank.

Those fingers squeezed a little more firmly. "We're almost there."

She nodded, even as her breath came in rapid gusts, as sweat trickled down her spine, as her pulse pounded in her veins.

Then they had arrived.

And her heart sank even deeper.

There wasn't any blood. This wasn't a broken bone. Nor was it an allergic reaction for her to cure. There wasn't . . . anything *anyone* could do.

She knew that in a single glance, sure as she saw the prone figure on the ground, Cody performing chest compressions.

Francis was gone.

Had probably been gone even before his body hit the earth.

Graham made a garbled noise, skidding to a stop next to her, his mind filled with such chaos and pain that for a moment, her breath was absolutely frozen in her lungs. Then she compartmentalized and got to work.

She grabbed the bag from Graham, dropped down next to Cody.

There was a defibrillator inside, and she had enough practice that it was strapped to Francis's chest in record time.

"Clear," she ordered.

Cody removed his hands.

The machine delivered the first shock. Then another.

To no avail.

She turned to Graham, readying to ask about a stretcher, but they were already opening one up, laying it next to her.

"Compressions again," she told Cody. "Let me know if you need a break."

He nodded, returning to CPR while she reached into the bag and began pulling out medication, even as her magic slid into his body, searching for the problem, knowing they were running out of time.

If his heart had truly given out, then there was nothing medically or magically she could do to save him.

She focused on finding a vein to rapidly start an IV, drawing the medicine into the syringe, then on administering it before they lifted Francis onto the stretcher. Cody knelt on top of it, continued with the compressions, even as the machine kept working in tandem. And all the while she was pouring more magic into Francis, pushing it through his body, searching his heart for deformities, his brain for blockages, his lungs for clots.

"Move," she said, beginning to lift the stretcher.

It flew out of her hands, Morgan and Mason grabbing it in tandem and hauling ass to the infirmary.

Her knees were weak. She was using vast amounts of magic to keep the blood flowing through Francis's body, to ensure his brain wasn't starved of oxygen. But she forced herself to focus on the next task, not what would happen if they failed. Instead, she just kept using her powers and took off after them, stumbling along the path.

She fell, scraping her knees, her palms, and then Graham was there, scooping her up.

"I—" she began, feeling his magic pouring into her brain.

"Save your strength," he said. "I have you."

Then he was running after Morgan and Mason, moving faster than she ever could, and she just concentrated on making sure oxygenated blood reached Francis's brain, on trying to stimulate his heart to beat.

She did that all the way to the infirmary.

Then continued to do it in the room.

Then kept with it as Gabby pumped fluids and hormones as the defibrillator kept administering shocks, as Cody was relieved by Morgan on CPR.

But every time she let the magic ease, pulled back to see if any of the medications or magic had worked, Francis's heart wouldn't start up, wouldn't take over, and he didn't regain consciousness.

And she knew.

She didn't want to admit it, didn't want to stop fighting.

But she knew that her initial assessment had been correct.

There was nothing they could do to bring Francis back.

Yes, they could exhaust themselves physically and mentally. Yes, they could keep moving his blood for him, continue providing oxygen to his brain.

But he wasn't coming back.

Her shoulders slipped the tiniest bit before she caught them. She didn't want to be the one to make this call, and yet at the same time, she knew she had to be the one to make it.

She was the most senior healer.

She had the most training.

She'd brought all of these additional technologies, gone to medical school for exactly this type of training, and for the most part, her people were healthier with that combination of technology and magic. But there were things even her mishmash of magic and tech couldn't make whole.

This was one of those things.

Which meant she had to do one of the hard things.

She had to call it.

Agony gripped her heart, making it feel as broken as Francis's, but she kept her shoulders straight as she released her powers, felt the blood slow in his body, pushed only by the rapid compressions Morgan was performing.

She moved toward him, touched his arm. "Stop."

He shook his head. "I'm not tired. I can—"

"*Stop*," she said, more firmly this time, squeezing his wrist, getting him to look at her. "There's nothing left we can do."

Her friend's eyes darkened with pain and all at once, she remembered that Francis had been like a father to him and his brothers after their father had been killed in the Dalshie attacks of the 1940s.

"We have to help him," he said. "We have to—"

There were tears in his eyes, and it was like a knife slicing through her own pain, making it cut even deeper, hurt somehow even more. Because it wasn't just her not being able to help her people, losing one of her own. Her inability to help Francis meant that her friends would hurt and suffer.

For a second, she dropped her hand from his arm, let her chin fall forward as he continued CPR.

She could try . . . something.

She could use more magic.

No. It wasn't going to help.

Graham's hand encircled her arm, his chest came up to press against her back, and then he said softly, "He's gone, Morg."

"No." Morgan kept going. "He's not. If we—"

Graham stepped to the side, releasing her arm and using both of his to pull Morgan away from Francis's body. "He's gone," he repeated. "He's gone."

Morgan fought him, struggling in Graham's hold for one long moment then he seemed to collapse from the inside out, falling away from the stretcher, sliding down to his knees, and the last thing Suz saw before he hunched over were the tears sliding down his face.

"Suz."

It was a choked-out sound that had her glancing up into the pain-filled eyes of Mason.

"I'm sorry," she whispered.

"It's n-not—" His lids slid closed, and he breathed deeply. "It's not your fault," he said softly.

She nodded, felt the pulse of agreement along the bond, Graham's pain banked, even as he sent reassuring vibes across their connection. But it didn't make her feel better. Not when Francis was there, was gone.

Not when she hadn't been able to save him.

This was the one thing she was good at. The *one* thing. She was crap at relationships, a mediocre friend, married to this fucking job.

And. She. Hadn't. Been. Able. To. Save. Him.

Her stomach twisted, bile burned the back of her throat.

She was going to throw up, and she knew she was going to do it in front of everyone unless she ran from this room, unless—

Gabby appeared in the doorway, blocking her single exit route.

Her face was drawn, heavy lines bracketing the outside of her mouth. "Is he—?"

Suz bolted, pushed past her, and sprinted for her office.

Francis was a teacher. *The* teacher. He'd helped every generation of Rengalla in recent history master their control of magic. He'd taught her how to heal, had encouraged her to go to medical school.

He hadn't just been a surrogate father to the Triplets.

He'd been one to her, to Gabby, to nearly everyone.

And Suz had let him die.

She barely felt the impact on her knees when she dropped

to the floor. Instead, she was overrun with retching, with her body expelling everything in her stomach from recent memory. Her throat burned as she heaved into the trash can, over and over and *over* again. Long after her stomach was empty. Long after she'd stopped bringing anything up, she continued to gag.

Until a cool cloth was placed on the back of her neck.

Until Graham's hand softly traced circles over her spine. He was speaking, but she didn't hear him for a long time, and then it took longer to actually tease apart the actual words he was speaking from the soft noise.

"Hush, baby," he was murmuring. "It'll be okay. Hush. Hush, now."

"I-I—" Then she was crying, or maybe she'd always been crying, but either way, she spun around and launched herself into his arms and lost it.

"I've got you, Firefly. It's okay. I'm here," he said, over and over.

She knew she needed to get it together. She needed to tell Francis's wife, Margaret. She had to prepare the body. She had—

Her eyes burned all over again, sobs bubbled in her chest.

One task.

She needed to focus on one task at a time.

She needed to be strong for everyone else.

And tonight, she could wallow in this dark feeling, in her failure, in the pain of not being able to save a man she had loved.

Had.

Fuck.

Soothing thoughts trailed down the bond, tried to comfort her, but she could feel Graham's pain beneath the gentle emotions. He was hurting. Because of her.

Deep breath.

One task.

She pushed out of his hold, firmly when he didn't immediately release her. "I need to take care of things," she said, moving to the small mirror in the corner, using a little magic to soothe the swelling and redness of her eyes and nose.

Strong.

She needed to shut the rest of this down and be strong.

"Suz—"

That kindness and sympathy in his tone wasn't helping her ability to stay strong, so she locked it down, tucked it away to focus on later.

"I need to talk to Margaret."

"Cody left to get her."

She nodded, stepped into the hall and walked back to the room that held her absolute worst nightmare.

But the nightmare would have to wait.

Because right now, her people needed her to be their healer.

And if she couldn't heal the body of a man who'd been like a father to so many, then God help her, she needed to make a start at healing their hearts.

FOURTEEN

Graham

SHE WAS GOING through the motions, pressing forward, the outer shell of her mind so damned cold that he might have wondered if she were sad at all. But he'd seen her in her office, throwing up repeatedly into the garbage, tears staining heavy tracks down her cheeks. He'd held her as she'd sobbed.

A broken, horrible sound.

Suz was hurting, just like the rest of them.

Maybe more than many of them.

And now she was holding Margaret, her arms wrapped tightly around the other woman as she cried and cried and cried.

He could feel Suz's exhaustion—physical *and* emotional, but after she'd taken those five minutes in her office, after she'd lost it behind closed doors, she'd become a pillar of strength. No tears, just gentle words and tight hugs, soft orders, and a calming presence.

But that calming wasn't working on Margaret any longer.

Grief seemed to have hit her all of a sudden. She'd gone

from silently holding Francis's hand to gut-wrenching screams, her pain a palpable wave in the room.

"Graham?"

He glanced up at the sound of Suz in his mind, met her gaze. Her mental voice was even, but brittle, as if the whole calm façade she was projecting would disappear in an instant if the wrong word was spoken or action was taken. *"What do you need?"* he asked, not delving beneath that mask, understanding instinctively that she needed it right now.

"I need a sedative for Margaret. Can you ask Dor to draw one up?"

He kept his eyes on hers and nodded then slipped out into the hall where Doreen was talking softly with Morgan and Mason. Monroe, their brother and the final of the Triplets, was off grounds on a mission, but he'd been notified and was en route.

"Dor?" he asked.

She turned to face him, pale beneath the golden hues of her skin, her eyes red. "Yes, honey?"

He tilted his head down the hall, indicating she should follow.

"What is it?" she asked.

"Suz asked for a sedative for Margaret. Can you draw one?"

"I'll do it right now."

Dor disappeared into the room and he turned to follow her, except at that moment, Monroe pushed through the door into the infirmary, his dark hair windblown and agony on his face. "It's not true," he said, glancing around the waiting room, the space having filled over the last hour with grieving Rengalla. "Tell me, it's not true!"

Morgan pushed off the wall, his eyes red but under control again. "Bro—"

"It's not—" Monroe shoved Morgan back. "Where is he? We just need to heal him and—"

Mason came close to his brothers, said something too softly for Graham to hear.

But Monroe's response was audible, his denials rising by the minute as he tried to push past his siblings and move down the hall.

"Why couldn't you save him?" he was shouting. "Why couldn't—"

Graham moved in, not about to let Suz hear him, not about to allow her to shoulder any more grief. He could already feel her guilt eating her alive, knew acutely they were the same in that aspect. If they considered someone theirs, it was agony to know they'd failed to keep their charge safe.

He'd not kept his—

No.

He couldn't go down that particular mental path, not when it was already so raw and exposed after seeing Francis like that in the field, body sprawled, face almost peaceful, and yet death all around.

That was too much like—

Enough.

Graham pushed that down, moved toward the Triplets, readying to order them to take it outside, but Gabby beat him there, taking Monroe's arm and leading him to the corner as she spoke softly into his ear. Morgan and Mason followed, and Graham knew they would lean on each other.

"You okay?" Cody asked. He had his arm around Daughtry's shoulders, her violet eyes swollen and red.

Okay wasn't a word he'd use to describe himself. "I need to go check on Suz."

Cody nodded and Graham started to slip by them, but Daughtry caught his arm. "Be careful with her," she said quietly. "Suz will blame herself a-and—" A shake of her head. "We all know that sometimes there just isn't any way to save someone."

The memories locked beneath that trapdoor in his mind threatened to burst free.

He knew that, had learned that lesson long before today.

"I'll take care of her."

Her smile was faint. "See that you do," she murmured. "I'll save my heavy threats about not hurting her for another day."

"Raincheck," he said lightly.

Amusement in her eyes. "Exactly." She tilted her head down the hall. "Now go. Cody and I will handle it out here."

Nodding his thanks, he didn't waste any time, instead moving back into the room, back to Suz, back to the pain that was threatening to overwhelm.

Margaret was in bed next to Francis. She'd been sedated and lay unconscious, her arms around him, her head on the pillow. Even asleep, her face showed her pain, lines gouging her forehead, cheeks, and mouth.

Dor and Suz were tucking a blanket around her, hands gentle as they smoothed back her hair, as they covered her tightly with that thin cotton.

"Go," Dor said. "I'll watch over her while you get some rest."

Suz shook her head. "I'm fine. I should—"

"*Go.*" Dor's eyes flashed. "I know I'm no longer the senior healer, but I'll make it an order if I have to. You're dead on your feet."

"I need to do *something*. I-I—"

Figuring this argument could go on a long while, Graham decided he'd heard enough. He crossed to Suz, scooped her up, and nodded at Dor. "Call us if you need anything."

She was fighting him, surprisingly strong—no, not *surpris-*

ingly strong. She was the epitome of the word, but it would have been nice if she were slightly less powerful, as he was trying to abscond with her for her own good.

Luckily, Cody and Dee had managed to clear out most of the waiting room, and the Triplets' mother had arrived, the trio along with Gabby, all talking quietly in the corner. Dee walked ahead of him to the door, ignoring the protests from Suz ("Put me down, you Neanderthal!" "Put me down *immediately*." "I need to—insert various task here."). Dee opened the door, held it wide as he carried Suz out into the hall, smiling approvingly, even as Suz's protests grew in volume.

"You need to put me down," she growled once they'd turned the corner, glaring at him with the full force of those chocolate brown eyes.

"I'll put you down."

But he didn't put her down, just kept walking to his quarters.

She huffed. "*When* will you put me down?" she snapped.

"When you're in bed."

"Graham!"

"Suz!"

She continued glaring.

"Look, baby," he said. "You can pretend with everyone else, but you can't pretend with me. I'm in your mind. I can feel that maelstrom you've got happening, and even if it was just you hurting"—which was unacceptable to him—"you're exhausted. You need to rest so that you can be there for everyone else when the hard stuff comes."

She fell quiet, and he could feel her turning his words over in her mind, wanting to discount them. In fact, searching for any angle that would allow her to do so.

Which meant that he needed to use a different tact.

But what would work?

Even now, he could feel her building an argument in his mind, preparing to demand he take her back.

He wouldn't, of course.

He could be just as stubborn.

He'd tie her to the bed or lock her in his room. He'd hand-cuff them together and—

"Stop with the kinky thoughts," she muttered.

Graham blinked. "What?"

"You're thinking of handcuffs and rope and locks." Her chin came up. "Well, I'm not into that, and even if I was, I need to get back to the infirmary and—"

He traced a finger down her nose. "Dor has it."

"I'm the senior healer. I need to be there."

"You need rest."

"I slept last night!"

"You used a boatload of magic today." He fixed her in place with a glare. "In fact, you used a boatload of *my* magic, too." So much that he was teetering on the edge of exhaustion himself. "You would be unconscious right now, if not for the bond. And you might very well end up that way if you keep pushing yourself once this adrenaline burst is over."

"I'm fine."

His temper snapped. "You're fine?" he asked, plunking her down on her feet. "You're *fine?*" He nudged her forward. "If you're so fine, why don't you walk your ass back to the infirmary?"

Her brows pulled together, but her nose was nearly in the elevation of Everest, it was lifted so high. "Fine," she gritted. "I will."

She spun, took one step—

And fell over.

Or she would have, if he hadn't caught her and swept her

back into his arms. "You still think you'll be of any use to anyone in this state?"

Her jaw clenched, but she didn't answer.

Which was fine by him. He just carried her back to his rooms, slamming his palm on the keypad to unlock the door then kicking the wooden panel closed behind him. He tossed her, probably too unceremoniously, onto his bed and prowled over to his dresser.

"Do I need to use these?" he snapped, holding up a pair of handcuffs. "Or can I trust that you'll keep your ass in bed while I go get you some food?"

She pushed herself up to a seated position, crossed her arms. "I'm—"

His temper hadn't magically stitched itself back together. "If you finish that statement with anything other than *planning to stay right where you put me.*" His words were sharp, too sharp. But she was hurting and exhausted and for fuck's sake, he need to take care of her. She needed nourishment and rest and—

"What?" She straightened but didn't get off the bed. "You'll do what?"

"I'll pull out my spare pair and handcuff your ankles, too."

Her eyes narrowed. "You wouldn't."

He lifted a brow. "Wouldn't I?"

Silence.

Her mind probed his, and he let the walls fall, let her see his determination, see how raw he felt, how this day's events had brought way too many things to the surface. But despite all of that, he was going to make sure she was okay.

And he had the handcuffs to prove his determination.

Finally, she sighed and kicked off her shoes.

"Fine," she muttered. "I'll stay here."

Relief rippled through him, and he took a breath to steady himself, grabbed on to his patience and control and said, "If you're still in bed when I get back, I'll tell you what Firefly means."

She was still glaring, but her mind softened against his. "I don't care."

He knelt by her side. "Don't you?"

A scowl. "No."

He brushed back her hair. "Should I bribe you instead with chocolate cake?"

Her lips pressed flat.

"A la mode?"

She sighed and shook her head. "I don't need the cake," she said. "If it puts you at ease, I'll stay in bed, Graham. I promise."

His heart swelled, and he kissed her lightly on the forehead. "Thank you."

"I reserve the right to pull these privileges on you, you know that, right?" she said.

He straightened. "And I reserve the right to be as stubborn as you."

A huff, but the corner of her mouth lifted, and her mind wasn't quite as bleak. "Go get the food, so we can eat." Her fingers ran along the edge of his jaw. "I can feel your exhaustion pulling at you."

More heart swelling. More love for this woman pooling deep inside, filling him up, making him know that the bond was the single thing he'd be most grateful for forever. It had made him see reason when he'd been so determined to stay away. And it had given him the motivation and avenue to wind his way to a future with this amazing woman.

She settled onto the mattress. He tugged the covers over her, set a T-shirt out on the nightstand for her to change into, in case she wanted to be more comfortable. Then he tilted his head toward the exit. "I'll be right back," he promised.

Her tone was dry, but her mind was still gentle against him. "I'll count the minutes."

Grinning, he turned for the hall, slipping quietly through the door.

And locking it behind him.

Because he may be in love with that woman inside the room.

But he wasn't stupid.

Especially when he heard the soft jiggle of the doorknob, the muttered curse through the panel.

"Bed," he ordered.

Turned out, she could make that adorable annoyed huff he loved to coax out of her, even across the bond.

FIFTEEN

Suz

THE KNOCK on the door had her looking up into the faces of the two people who never came to the infirmary.

Her parents.

She closed the file on her computer and stood up. "H-hi. Come in."

Her mom kissed her on the cheek, grabbed her arms and said, "You look good, baby."

She didn't.

She couldn't possibly.

It had been one day since Francis—a dart of pain shot through her heart—since he'd died, and she was a mess, trying to do too many things, yet unable to stop. Because if she stopped . . .

She *couldn't* stop.

Or else she would think, and then where would that get her? It would get her *here* with stinging eyes, a churning stomach, and a tongue that felt thick and furry and useless.

The bond in her mind pulsed, filling her with Graham's gentle presence.

And she could breathe.

Could look at her parents without bursting into tears.

They sat silently in front of her desk, her mom taking the chair, her dad standing next to her shoulder, and both of them studying her closely.

"Come here, baby."

Suz moved around the desk, knelt in front of her, alarm blipping through her. "Is everything okay?"

Her mom shifted, grabbing Suz's hand, clasping it tightly. Suz's eyes slid closed, feeling like a child again. Those warm, slightly-calloused fingers grasping hers, making her feel like everything would be okay, like the world was a kind, safe place and—

She shifted, knowing that was a fanciful thought.

The world could be cruel for those without protection.

It could teach a lesson as easily as the sun set and the ocean pounded against rocks.

Without fail.

Her mom released her hand, studying her closely. "I thought you'd come to us."

Suz felt a bolt of guilt. "I'm sorry," she whispered. "Everything happened so fast, and then I've been helping Margaret make arrangements and—"

"Not about Francis," her dad said.

"Though we were so sorry to hear of his passing." Her mom patted Suz's knee. "Everyone knows that you did absolutely everything to try and help him, of course. But sometimes it's a person's time and—"

Suz turned away, crossed back behind the desk.

Someone's time.

God, she'd heard that way too many times over the last twenty-four hours.

"You did everything you could."

"It's not your fault."

And if not hers, then whose?

She was the head healer, she was the one who was supposed to know that his heart was failing. If she'd caught it and healed him sooner—

Graham in her mind again, stepping between those thoughts and batting them away. *"Enough,"* he murmured along the bond, his mental voice faint as he was taking a shift on the far side of the Colony. *"This does no one—especially you—any good."*

She didn't have a response to that.

How could she?

She'd counseled many a person to let go of their guilt, to not let it eat at them, to drag them down. But . . . it wasn't so easy, was it? How could it be? Not when the thoughts kept coming, not when she continued to relive every decision and the consequences.

The if-onlys were real and heavy.

So, the guilt persisted.

"We thought you'd have come to us." Her mom slanted a look up at Suz's dad, who nodded.

"About what?"

A pause. "About the fact that you've bonded."

Suz blinked. Then sank into her chair. "Oh."

"We didn't," her dad said, "expect to have to track you down to discuss the bonding."

Why did *the bonding* sound so ominous?

"Oh," she said again, not sure where this was going. It definitely didn't seem like an appropriate time to have this conversation, let alone to be discussing it like she'd been led off to the gallows.

Did they not want her to be bonded?

To most, it was like winning the lottery.

Maybe they thought it was too sudden or didn't like Graham. No. They adored Graham, had always referred to him as their son when she and Amelia had been glued at the hip.

So, maybe they thought—

Her heart sank.

Because maybe they thought that Suz wasn't the right person for him.

And if *they* thought that, then the rest of the Colony—

No.

That was the guilt talking and the emotion of the last day and . . . it wasn't her. She was worthy to have someone as great as Graham.

"Glad you came to . . ." His mental voice blanked out, their connection not yet strong enough to sustain prolonged contact over this distance. *". . . that conclusion without me . . ."*

Her heart squeezed. *"I'm guessing the rest of that was a threat to beat it into me. But if you can hear this, go back to work. I'm okay."*

A brush of his mind along hers. *". . . later."*

"Not that I'm not happy about it, love."

She blinked, focused on her mom and dad, on the conversation in front of her rather than the one in her head. "What?"

"We're happy you bonded," her father said.

"Just surprised we didn't hear it from you," her mother added.

"I—"

"Don't use work as an excuse," her mom said, and not particularly unkindly. But it was said firmly.

Suz felt her shoulders slump.

"We're thrilled for you, darling. It's a good thing, and Graham is a good man," she said. "I think you two will be very happy together."

"If I don't drive him away like I did every other male I'd ever dated."

There's a special kind of silence for blurted-out words a person intended to keep in their mind. It descends heavy and stifling, until the room's occupants can feel it, until it begins to suck out the oxygen and makes cheeks burn in embarrassment.

That was the type of silence that filled the room.

That was the type of silence that made her fingers twitch, ache to retrieve the roll of duct tape she kept in the bottom drawer of her desk and slap some over her mouth.

It was also the type of silence that had her father excusing himself from the room, closing the door softly behind him.

Leaving her with her mother.

And the urge to upchuck and run away screaming in equal measures.

But she didn't.

Suz was made of sterner stuff.

"Why would you drive him away?" her mother asked, an interminable amount of time later.

She knew she had two choices—commit to that running away screaming urge. Or bluff her way through the rest of this conversation. "That didn't come out like I intended," she said.

"Hmm."

"I just meant that I'm really busy with work a lot, and I get pulled in a lot of directions." She stood and gestured toward the large whiteboard that hung on the back wall of her office. There was a myriad of tasks she needed to accomplish. "Dating me isn't like dating a normal Rengalla. I can't just push off a critical case because I want to sleep in or go on a dinner date. I have to be ready at the drop of a hat."

"Or, you could get more help," her mom said softly. "Dante gave you the budget for more healers when the Rengalla were recalled from the satellite bases. With us all under one roof, you have more patients than you can handle."

"There's no one qualified enough." Healing was a rare gift among the Rengalla.

"Then train those with the ability."

Suz swallowed. "No one aside from Gabby has been interested."

Silence.

Not borne of embarrassment this time. But rather of disappointment. Which felt awesome. She loved disappointing the person who'd given birth to her, raised her, who'd loved her unconditionally.

Good times.

"I don't think that's quite true, my love," her mom said. "But it is a convenient excuse."

"What is?"

"To make sure you're understaffed. To ensure that you're so busy, you don't have to ever let someone get close." Her mom shook her head, lips turned up ever so slightly at the corners. "It's the perfect barrier between you and everyone else."

Suz sucked in a breath.

"The difficult thing, honey, and I'm only saying this because I love you, but I think the bond magic chose you because you are so closed off to romantic love. Oh, I know you date and say you want a relationship," she added when Suz began to protest, "but that's not true, is it?"

Her throat was tight, words stoppered up in the back of it. She shook her head.

She wanted a relationship and a family, more than anything else.

It was just . . .

"Or, even if it is true." Her mom stood, moved toward Suz. "If you do want someone to love, someone who loves you, you're too scared to let someone in deep enough to make that a possibility." Her eyes went wide, understanding dawning. "You're too scared that they'll hurt you." A beat. "Like someone else hurt you."

Suz shook her head. "No, that's not it. I'm fine. I'm just busy and it's a lot and I'm upset about Francis."

All true.

Just not the whole truth.

For a long time they stood a foot apart, quietly staring at each other. Then her mom wrapped her arms around Suz and held her tight. "It's okay, baby. You don't have to tell me. But I know that things with you and Graham will work out fine."

Suz couldn't find it in herself to muster another denial.

She just let her mom hug her.

And hoped that she was right.

SIXTEEN

Graham

HE HUNG UP HIS GEAR, went to his quarters for a quick shower, then went to the infirmary to retrieve Suz.

He could see this becoming a pattern.

One he would be very happy to repeat day in and day out.

Especially if he could tempt her away with a kiss.

Grinning, he didn't notice Morgan until it was too late. He nearly mowed his friend down, and one look at his face told Graham all he needed to know about Morgan's mental state.

Terrible jokes, plenty of sarcasm, and the persistence of an annoying gnat.

That was Morgan.

Not this shell of a man, his normally tan skin pale, his eyes bloodshot, his spatial awareness totally obliterated.

And he reeked of booze.

Was so far gone, he was teetering on his feet.

"Hey, man," Graham said, grabbing his arm and steadying him.

"Graham-man," Morgan slurred. "Heh. That rhymes."

"No, it doesn't," Graham said.

"Graham, man, slam, tam"—a hiccup—"ma'am, ham, slam—wait, did I say that already?"

"You're rhyming skills while inebriated aren't great," he pointed out.

"Greater than sitting around sober and thinking." Morgan pointed at his temple, nearly poked his eye out in the process. "I *can't* think. I can't sit around and think about . . ." A shake of his head and Graham had to brace himself so they both didn't fall over. The man was fucking heavier than he looked. "Now, let me go."

"Let you go where?"

Morgan's expression clouded. "I want to go."

"Where?" Graham asked.

Morgan shoved him off, staggered a few steps down the hall. "I want to go!"

"Fuck," he muttered, moving after him. Drunk was one thing. Hell, Graham had drunk an extra beer himself the night before, feeling the dark pall of Francis's death, wanting to be a little looser and lighter and—

"I want to go!"

Morgan's eyes were hazed and angry, even as he wavered like they were on a ship during a storm, rather than the perfectly level floor inside the Colony.

"So, let's go," Graham told him. "I'll walk you wherever you need to go."

A nod that nearly sent Morgan to the ground. "'kay."

He took his friend's arm again and let Morg lead them on a wavering path toward . . . *oh shit.*

The armory.

Well, that wasn't going to work for him.

The LexTal was a crack shot, all of them were, but not

under the influence of what appeared to be an entire barrel of whiskey.

"Hey," Graham said, slowing their pace. "Maybe we should get some coffee or something first. You wouldn't want to—"

"I'm going," Morg slurred. "I'm fucking going."

Okay, he'd tried to play nice. He knew his friend was hurting, that losing Francis had been like losing a father. And having felt that painful loss himself, he understood how it could drive someone off the rails.

But . . . Graham wasn't going to let him risk hurting himself or someone else.

Morgan would thank him for it when he sobered up.

Probably.

Maybe.

Either way, he wasn't letting him anywhere near a gun.

"You're not going in there, man. Let's hit the gym," he said, trying for distraction. "I'll even let you beat me up."

"I"—a sharp shake of his head—"don't want. Want to shoot something. Want—"

"It's not happening."

Lost hazel eyes on him for a moment then they hardened, filled with fury.

Graham was ready for Morg when he came at him. His friend was a skilled fighter, but so was Graham, and he had the benefit of being sober. Which meant he was able to feint to the side and grab Morgan's arm, twisting it and holding him in place.

"Better yet," he grunted, taking an elbow in the gut before he managed to grip the other arm. "Why don't we skip the shooting *and* the ass-kicking and go straight to the sleeping off portion of the evening?"

"Fuck you."

"No, thanks. I've got a woman to do that for me," Graham said lightly, loving that it was the truth.

Morgan wasn't drunk enough to miss that fact either.

"Fucking bonding. Fucking happy couples. Fucking world is so fucking fucked and—"

"And I think you've reached your quota on f-bombs for the day."

Not his voice.

A woman's.

Graham glanced up to see Darcy shaking her head, her lips pressed flat. She acknowledged him with a nod but didn't otherwise say anything to him. Nope. That was all reserved for Morgan.

"What the fuck are you doing?" she snapped, her gaze locked onto the drunkard's face.

"Getting drunk," Morgan muttered. "Shooting shit."

Pale brown eyes drifted up to Graham's, one black brow lifted in question.

Still holding Morg, he shrugged. "We had a disagreement about the intelligence of doing the second."

"Hmm." Seemingly warring with herself, she tapped a finger to a bright red lip, tapped the toe of her heavy combat boot. "Bring him with me," she said after a moment. "I'll sober him up, make sure he stays out of trouble. I'm sure you want to get to Suz."

"I don't *want* to go with her," Morgan whined before he could reply. "She's *mean*."

"Mean seems to be what you need right now," Darcy said.

"I do want to get to Suz," Graham said. "But I don't want to leave you with him when he's like this."

She waved a hand, turned and started walking down the hall, tossing over her shoulder, "I'll put him to rights. I've got loads of experience handling unruly drunks."

Morgan groaned.

"It's for the best, buddy," Graham said.

"No," Morgan said morosely. "It's for the worst."

"Why?"

"She's got loads of experience handling *me*," he said, groaning again.

Graham chuckled. "Sounds like she's better suited for keeping you in line than I am then."

"You got him, or you need help?" Darcy called.

"I've—" Graham tightened his grip when Morgan tried to make a break for it. "Lead the way," he called back. "We're right behind you."

Then he frog-marched his friend down the hall and to a small suite of rooms that were decorated with a surprisingly softly feminine touch, considering the punk-rock look Darcy sported.

"It's not him, really," she murmured, once they'd dumped a now nearly comatose Morgan into bed and wrestled off his shoes.

"I know," he assured her. "He lost a father."

"Yes." She tucked the blankets up and over Morgan's snoring body. "Twice now."

"I know." He nodded, his own dual loss threatening to leave the confines of his mind. First, the blow from the death of the man, of his own father. Then the impact of the death of the family—or perhaps worse, the death of his confidence that he had the ability to keep it all together.

Either way, it had been hell.

But it didn't have any impact on the present.

He'd navigated them through, they were all at a good place.

Plus, now he had Suz.

He could finally, *finally* shut the door on the past.

Forever.

SEVENTEEN

Suz

"YOU KNOW," she said, a week later, "you never did tell me what Firefly means."

"I didn't?" Graham asked innocently.

She smacked him lightly across the arm. "You know you didn't."

He smirked. "It's not my fault you were asleep when I got back."

"You could have told me when I woke up."

A nod. "I could have."

Annoyed, she pressed her lips flat. This week had been absolute hell. She'd fallen asleep after Graham had locked her in his room, but well before he'd returned with the promised chocolate cake. And by the time she'd woken, she'd needed to get to the infirmary.

The cake had been stowed in her fridge. The sandwich had been scarfed.

And Graham had been gone.

Gone, but not forgotten.

Ha.

But seriously, how could she have forgotten? She'd woken in his bed, her body covered in one of his T-shirts, the fresh forest scent of him covering her from head to toe. And she'd woken up knowing exactly where she was. No startling awake, wondering where she'd slept and then remembering the events. Nope. Her lids had slowly peeled back, and she'd *known*.

She was with Graham.

Or she had been for several hours, at least.

Last night, however, he hadn't warmed her bed, even for a few hours. He kissed her at the door then left to pull a night shift. But his presence *was* heavy in her mind, not smothering exactly, but warm and comforting, like the super expensive but fluffy comforter she had on her bed.

She showered quickly, saw that a donut and peony had magically appeared during her rest, along with a note that was folded neatly next to it.

Instead of reading it right away, she slipped that piece of paper into her pocket, knowing she needed to focus on work and solely work, knowing that after this tough week, she was at risk of collapse. But she couldn't collapse. Not yet. Her people still needed a healer. Not a woman who missed a man who'd been a mentor to so many. Not heartbroken or guilt-ridden or sad.

All of that could come later.

Today, her people still needed her.

So, she went to the infirmary. And then she did her job.

With that paper in her pocket, an insignificant weight in reality, but in her mind, it was solid and steady, and throughout the next hours, she found herself reaching into her pocket and fingering the folded edge, taking comfort in a piece of paper that had her name on the front of it but might have absolutely nothing of importance on the inside.

But it had helped.

She was there to treat the twisted ankle, available to slip away and see Margaret when the other woman was overwhelmed with the funeral arrangements. She'd encouraged her to lie down, helped coax her into sleep. Then after, Suz had finished the funeral arrangements and had arranged a schedule of visitors at regular intervals to visit with Margaret and make sure she ate.

That had taken hours, and by the time Graham had reappeared in the infirmary later that night, leading her out with hardly a word, she'd been exhausted all over again.

She hadn't made a protest when he'd weaved their fingers together, just let him take her back to his rooms.

To his bed.

Into his arms.

Then, she'd slept in his arms.

The days that followed didn't get any easier.

They buried Francis. They made arrangements for his students to talk with counselors, found replacement teachers.

But the hole in all their hearts wasn't closed, and it wouldn't be for a long time.

"Hey," Graham murmured, running a finger over her cheek. "It'll get better."

She shifted so she could face him, tearing her eyes off the gorgeous greenery that filled his little hideaway. He'd ferreted her here for lunch, and Suz wasn't going to complain, not when the walls of the infirmary felt like they were closing in on her. That itchy feeling had been growing all week, telling her she was missing something.

Was it something she hadn't done but should have?

Something that would have saved Francis?

Some piece of medical history that she'd ignored to his peril?

Or was it something else? Something that had nothing to do with the death and her inability to keep him safe.

She didn't know, or at least, she couldn't yet figure it out.

Either way, she'd been ecstatic to get away, to try and clear her head, and to be with Graham.

"You were busy this week," she said, changing the subject, not wanting to think about Francis, just for a little bit.

He nodded. "I know. I'm sorry I wasn't able to see you as much as I'd wanted."

She *hadn't* seen him much. Just at meal times since that night and when he'd walked her back to her rooms when it got late. In fact, if he weren't in her mind, she might have chalked it up to him having become disinterested, assumed her difficulty with being loved was rearing its ugly head.

But he was there in her mind.

Steady and warm and *there*.

Even if he wasn't *physically* there.

Hmm.

She shifted a little further, changing their position from side-by-side so she could face him, and for the first time in a week, the haze of grief cleared enough for her to truly see his face.

She noticed the dark circles beneath and deep lines surrounding his eyes. His skin slightly pale, his normally clean-shaven face dotted with stubble. But his mouth was curved into his normal Graham smile, his touch was gentle, his tone was perfectly normal and laced with his typical light teasing.

Her healer instincts prickled.

And finally, she removed herself enough from her own pain to truly see what was *beneath* that face.

And beneath the carefully curated thoughts in his mind.

He was hurting.

Deeply.

She'd missed it.

So wrapped up in her own thoughts and tragedy and responsibility, she'd neglected to look deeper at the one person she should be most connected to.

Fuck.

Lifting her palm, she cupped his cheek. "What about you? Are you okay?"

He smiled. "I'm fine." But he retreated from her touch. Not in an abrupt movement that grabbed her attention. Instead, it was a subtle drawing back, the barest shift, and paired with a statement designed to distract. "You should eat something before duty calls," he said. "I already bought you those bigger jeans, now I need to get you to fit in them."

She snorted but didn't otherwise bite.

She did, however, do some shifting of her own.

Shifting so she could plunk herself down into Graham's lap and wind her arms around his neck. "Tell me what's up, Crumbles."

His brow lifted. His hips arched slightly. "Do you really want to know?"

She *did* want to know or wanted to feel what was *up* and pressing against the inside of her thigh. She certainly wanted a repeat of that night in her office, of the pleasure and the orgasms and the deliciousness of his muscled, gorgeous body. But she'd also caught the thread of pain beneath the innuendo and paired with the dark circles, the heavy lines, the careful distance he'd sneakily managed to erect, and Suz knew the most important thing in building this connection wasn't passion.

It was care and understanding and not accepting face value as truth.

So she didn't grind against him, didn't take that next step

that would have them both naked and him hard and hot inside her. "You're very good at keeping people at a distance, aren't you?"

That brow dropped, his lips curved into a sexy smirk, and his tone, though still light, had an undercurrent laced in it.

Of fear.

"I don't want to keep you at a distance." Heat slid into his eyes, blazed across the bond, as his hands dropped to her waist and he tugged her closer. "I want you close."

"Graham."

He lowered his head, trailed his mouth across her jaw, nipping lightly. "*Very* close."

It felt good. God, how it felt good to have him touching her. Not just because she felt pleasure at his touch—newsflash: she clearly did, the man had some serious skills—but it also felt incredible because she felt *his* pleasure, too.

Sliding along the bond, filling her while her nerve endings tap-danced with desire, with need.

Easy—it would be so easy to let that thread beneath his pleasure go, to ignore the bigger picture for the immediate gratification. He would make them both feel good and then they could just keep enjoying each other.

Except . . . she didn't want to enjoy him.

Or not *only* enjoy him.

She wanted to know him, to understand what made the shadows appear in his eyes, the pain that had him retreating.

She wanted—no *needed* to care for him as much as he'd cared for her.

Because this week he'd continued to bring her meals, to make sure she got enough rest. Every one of her physical needs had been met.

Not that he hadn't tried to emotionally help.

It just wasn't always that easy to heal a rift inside someone, especially when it was so raw and gaping.

But even if he couldn't take that pain away, he'd been there for her, in her mind, steady and warm and comforting. He was doing all the comforting. He was doing all the caring. He was leading their relationship down the path he wanted while she was too scared to truly be herself.

All because it was lovely to have someone look after her.

But she wasn't a fucking puppy.

She wouldn't fully be satisfied with meals and a walk once a day.

No, she wouldn't be. But deep down—and this was the hard part to admit—she was scared, terrified, on razor's edge. Because she was worried that Graham was going to look too close and find her wanting, and she would have shared too many parts of herself with him to reassemble all of the pieces back into herself.

He had the potential to change her, to shift those pieces, to form an entirely different puzzle.

And for a woman who'd spent much of her life only sharing the pieces she was willing to part with, this wasn't ideal.

But she wasn't by herself anymore, was she?

They were linked, permanently, and though it was a daunting prospect, that lifelong connection, she didn't think either of them truly ever considered not working at the bond, not making it something that centered them both.

To do that, she needed in.

To do that, she needed to let *him* in.

"I told you before that I'm not an easy woman to love." His face clouded, his mind flaring with anger at her words, but she simply placed a finger over his lips and continued. "But I didn't tell you why I know that it's true."

His mouth parted, hot breath glazing her finger, but he didn't try to speak over her, just watched her closely with those deep golden eyes.

"My parents love each other. I had good friends"—she smiled—"most especially Amelia growing up and Daughtry and Gabby now, not that I don't love Amelia, it's just—" She faltered.

He peeled her finger away, cupped her hand between both of his. "You just grew apart."

Suz smiled. "Yes." A sigh. "We still talk regularly and grab a meal once a month, but we've changed, and it's not the same as it was when we were spending every waking moment together."

"That's normal, don't you think?"

"Yes, I do. People grow apart, but"—she pushed to her feet —"I guess my point in me telling you this isn't that I have a bad story. I'm not like Dee or Gabby. I don't have trauma."

He stood too. "I'm glad you don't have trauma, Firefly. I don't want you hurt."

"But the thing is . . . God, this sounds so stupid."

"Tell me."

Her eyes narrowed at the order. "I'm intending to," she muttered. "That's why I brought it up in the first place."

The corners of his mouth twitched, but he didn't comment.

And she found herself back to talking, trying to organize her thoughts, trying to figure out how to communicate the truth she felt in her heart in some way that made even the slightest bit of sense.

"I keep people at a distance."

His mouth flattened.

"I've gotten really good at it over the years, especially after —" She hesitated, wanting him to know everything about her but hating how critically embarrassing this next part of her story was.

"After what?" he asked, a thread of fury in his voice.

"It's nothing horrible," she hurried to assure him. "I was just a young girl who got her heart broken. It's not like I'm uniquely qualified to expound on that phenomenon." She punched him lightly on the shoulder. "I would also venture to guess that you've left a few broken hearts behind your wake." A shrug. "It's a rite of passage into adulthood."

He tucked a strand of hair behind her ear. "So, why do I feel like the other shoe is about to drop, and a big one at that?"

"Because . . . it is, I guess." Then, knowing there would never be any easy way to describe exactly what had happened to pull the inner core of her so deeply behind her protective walls, she just blurted it out. "I fell in love with my residency advisor in Boston."

His mind blipped in confusion and she had to admit, the bond was convenient when it came to streamlining conversations.

"He was my boss after medical school, when I worked my way through my residency."

"I see."

She sighed, because no, he didn't. Not yet, anyway.

"He wasn't much older than me. Only four years, but he was a genius—and I don't use that term facetiously. He was the smartest person I had ever met, and I'd met a shit-ton of smart people during my years in medical school." Her lips pressed flat for a moment. "Well, he was gorgeous and smart, and a very talented neurosurgeon, and I fell hard. He liked me, too." Or so she'd thought, because next was the critically embarrassing part. "For the entire rotation, we spent our shifts together. Sixteen, eighteen, sometimes twenty-hour days. Me absorbing every bit of knowledge, and him talking cases through with me, teaching me new techniques, helping me look deep beneath the obvious issues to find the underlying problems beneath." She nibbled at the corner of her mouth. "He talked to me like an equal, and I just knew that he was the man I needed to spend the rest of my life with."

Graham released a slow breath.

"I know," she whispered. "I know it would have been impossible, even if things hadn't ended the way they had."

"That sounds ominous."

Suz let her gaze drift to the trees, to the lovely purple flowers this man had grown with his care. The memories were painful, but she supposed the entire painful experience was positive, at least for something.

It showed her that a good man was in front of her.

She turned back to him. "I met his wife." A bolt of surprise slid across the bond, but she kept going. "She came to warn me. I guess word had gotten around that I was the newest conquest." Her eyes held his, even though after all these years, her mortification was still acute. "Apparently, he liked to pick a young, reasonably attractive girl every rotation. He'd"—she made air quotes—"take them under his wing, help them learn the ropes, and then they'd go, and he'd move onto the next." Suz shook her head. "The worst part is that he was a great teacher. I learned so freaking much, but it was all . . . tainted, you know? I couldn't separate the two in my head, and everyone *knew*. They all knew I'd slept with a married man, that I'd been stupid enough to not realize I was being used. God, even now, it's just . . . so embarrassing."

"Suz."

Spinning, she moved to the tree, traced her fingers down the smooth bark. "I should have known, but I didn't, and I was so infatuated that I didn't put the pieces together. I had to be pulled aside and told—"

He covered her hand with his palm, leaned his chest against her back. "How could you have known?"

Slowly, she turned to face him, acknowledging the truth that had left her feeling too fucking vulnerable even after all these years. "Logically, there wasn't any way. I've gone over it too many times to count. He didn't wear a wedding ring or mention a family. None of the other staff members ever talked about him being married or about his wife. There were no photographs on his desk, and the hours we worked . . . well, they were insane. I was barely upright, let alone able to have a personal life outside of the hospital—"

Graham stepped close. "So, how could you possibly be to blame for that? He should have been upfront, he shouldn't have taken advantage of you, and he sure as shit shouldn't have been married while doing it."

"That's true," she admitted. "But I couldn't control him. I could only control *me*. And I'd always been so comfortable in myself, confident of my place in the world, that I was smart and talented and would make the right decision." A sigh as his hand came up to cup the back of her head. "Don't you see?"

"Your confidence was dinged."

"No," she said. "It was fucking steam-rolled. I couldn't trust myself any longer, couldn't be sure of my choices. I had been manipulated and therefore was vulnerable." Frustratingly, her eyes stung, but Suz had long since been past shedding tears for the bastard.

"I'm sorry," Graham murmured.

"Me, too," she said. "But I didn't tell you this so you'd feel bad for me. I want you to understand why I pull back sometimes, why I know it's hard to love me. I'm so walled up at times that it's not easy to get in." She touched her temple. "But you're *already* in, and as scary as that was at first, these last couple of weeks have taught me that I like you there. And I want you to know that I'm glad about the bond, glad that we have this chance together."

His half of their connection throbbed with emotion, a flurry that was so rapid she couldn't discern the individual threads of his feelings, could just sense their almost painful intensity.

"I'm terrified," she told him. "Scared I'll do something to mess this up. Scared you'll see something in my head and not look at me the way you're doing now—"

"Never." He dragged her head toward his, slanted his mouth across hers and kissed her until her head was spinning and her pulse pounding in her veins. "Never," he said again.

"But a man I loved lost his life this week, and I realized that even though I'm so fucking scared of screwing this up, I have to try. I have to *live*." She swallowed hard. "So, I'm going to try. I'm going to *live*. I've accepted that you're inside me, that I don't want to build a barrier around you and all of the memories and hopes and dreams deep inside."

"Suz—"

"I want *you*, Graham," she said, needing to get this out. "And I need you to know that I understand how precious this is between us, that I hope, I truly *hope* that we can get to the point where we have something like Cody and Dee, like Gabby and Mason, like John and Alex." Her lips brushed his. "Because if we can get there, we'll be two of the luckiest people on the planet."

His golden eyes were molten metal, his hand in her hair tightened, and then his lips found hers again.

She could still feel his pain as he kissed her, still sense that underlying thread of darkness that was hurting him, but it wasn't her place to push, not yet anyway. Give first. Give as much as she could. Be open, even though it was scary. Be strong, because that would mean he could rely on her strength when he was feeling weak.

And then she could be there.

For him.

Every piece of him.

Forever.

EIGHTEEN

Graham

HE KISSED her like the world was ending, his hands moving fiercely over her body, tearing off her shirt, pushing down her pants, dragging his lips along her jaw and down her throat.

She hissed out a breath, fingers clenching in his shirt when he sucked her nipple through her bra, and he used the bond ruthlessly, arrowing in on her pleasure, perfecting the pressure, the angle, the speed, reducing the woman he loved into a writhing pile of need as he paid homage to her glorious breasts.

But she wasn't the only one reduced.

He was shocked that he wasn't in flames. That he wasn't burned up and turned to ash.

Then he wasn't thinking about getting smaller, because he was between her thighs, and the need grew. Hers fed his. His fed hers. They merged and multiplied, growing exponentially until he felt as though he were the one who might fly over the precipice.

"*Now,*" she ordered, and they were so intertwined that he

wasn't certain if it was spoken across the bond or aloud. Not that it mattered.

He needed her.

He needed to love her, to worship her, to make her feel incredible.

Because he understood the gift she'd given him. He had felt how hard it had been for her to unearth that vulnerability, to reveal it to him. Just as he knew that he'd need to do the same, that the bond wouldn't work if it was only one of them ripping off the emotional Band-Aid.

Graham needed to tell her everything.

Just . . . not now.

Not when her body was a siren's call, when her need blazed within him and threatened to turn them both to cinders, not when she needed him to love her.

To *love* her.

That was a done deal. Probably had been a done deal well before he'd recognized the signs.

The bond had made him realize that much.

Keeping away hadn't done either of them any good in the end. Because when a person found the other half of their soul, there wasn't any force that could keep them apart.

The sun rose and set by Suz. His heart beat in order to care for hers. He would be her shield, her rock, her bolster when things were hard.

And they would be fucking incredible together.

They would be like Cody and Dee, like Mason and Gabby, like Alex and John.

They would be those lucky few.

"Now, Graham," Suz ordered again, but this time she didn't wait idly by. She pushed him to his back, climbed on top, and took him deep inside.

Bliss.

Perfect, absolute bliss.

That other half coming home. That final missing piece completing him. That . . . hell, it was every romantic thought that flitted through his mind, nonsensical but intense. Nirvana and somehow also soul-deep with notes of absolute perfection. All the words and feelings . . . at least until his brain no longer worked, until even those half-baked thoughts could hardly form, until he could do nothing but feel his mate on top of him, surrounding him, *inside* him.

And that was still perfect.

They moved like they were born to be together.

Perhaps they were.

They climbed the peak, holding each other tightly, flames licking at their heels, curling along their spines, sending their nerves firing, desire pooling in their stomachs. They hurtled toward the cliff, toward the pleasure that would incinerate them both.

And then they were airborne.

Floating through the clouds and slowly descending, their sweat-sheened bodies pressed tightly together, their limbs intertwined. Sunshine trickled through the clouds, dappling her skin with specks of gold.

She was beautiful and still perfect and still absolute bliss.

Smiling, he let his eyes slide closed, the exhaustion of this emotional week catching up with him, feeling Suz slip toward sleep right alongside him.

Summoning a herculean effort, he flicked a gaze toward the door, made sure the lock was engaged, then pulled the edge of the blanket they'd been sitting on around them.

Then he let sleep rise up, the perfection of his mate still glorious in his mind as he slipped off into oblivion.

This will never be perfect unless your deepest secrets are exposed, too.

His eyes flared open, his brain unable to distinguish if the thought had trickled from Suz's slumbering one or originated from his own.

Panic bubbled in his throat.

Sleep was forgotten.

Because Graham knew the words were true.

HE KNOCKED ON THE DOOR, dreading the conversation that had to happen, but knowing it needed to take place anyway.

He'd let this go on too long and now, the burden of that truth sat heavy in his gut, his heart, but . . . he needed to make sure. He had to protect—

The door opened to reveal a beautiful woman who, in the non-magical world, would look to be in her early forties. Her pale blonde hair was pulled back neatly. "Graham!" she exclaimed, sweeping toward him and pulling him into a hug. "This isn't a normal day for you to come and visit."

"I needed to talk with you," he said, careful to keep his tone even.

Always careful.

Always needing to be gentle and soft and even.

Otherwise—

She pulled back, her deep gray eyes staring deeply into his. "Yes," she murmured, "I think you do." A nod toward her rooms. "Why don't you come inside, and I'll make us a cup of tea?"

He despised tea, but he just let her lead him into the small kitchen the family suites all had. His mother had chosen cheery yellow cabinets with pale gray countertops, and everything was neatly stored, those counters gleaming.

She liked order.

After . . . she had needed it in order to function.

After . . . she had melted down if a spoon wasn't nestled properly into the others, if there was a crumb in the sink, a fingerprint on the fridge.

After, it had been the thing she'd clung to.

That and him.

She bustled around for several minutes, pulling the teapot out of a drawer, filling it with water before setting it on the stove, retrieving cups and saucers, sugar and cream, putting a plate full of cookies on the counter in front of him, along with a napkin. Action, busy, rapid actions followed by wiping and cleaning, a flurry that would make him dizzy if he paid attention to it.

Instead, decades had given him coping skills.

He couldn't make this part right, couldn't ease her anxiety. But he could eat carefully over the plate, could make sure those crumbs didn't end up on the counter, or God forbid, the floor. He could be quiet and still as she bustled. He could sit still and not shift the chair so as not to bring them out of the alignment she preferred.

Tiny things.

Small ways to protect.

Even when it wouldn't make a difference in the end.

Because when he left, she'd be a flurry of cleaning, a frenzy of wiping and dusting and scrubbing, of making certain everything was sanitary and clean, clean, *clean*.

It all had to be clean.

And that was just her inside. Outside, she was scared of bees, terrified of the wildlife surrounding the Colony, worried the dirt would contain an ancient pathogen that someone might unearth, panicked by the UV radiation coming from the sun, and the list went on.

She didn't live her life.

She meandered her way, frightened by any and all obstacles that might come her way.

His father had lain dying on that battlefield, Graham having fought by his side, a young soldier, so confident they'd win against the Dalshie and yet such a naïve idiot about what losses that victory would bring. He'd held his father's hand, watching the blood pool around him, magical burns covering his body, their healer trying desperately to save their people but unable to help them all, and he'd made his father a promise.

To look after Amelia—so tiny and vulnerable.

And to look after his mother.

He had promised his father that he wouldn't let her live like this, wouldn't allow her to be ruled by anxiety, that she would have a full and happy life.

Graham had failed.

She had him and Amelia. She had her knitting and her transcription work. But she didn't have friends. She didn't leave these quarters unless he or Amelia was with her. She didn't go outside unless he cajoled her into it.

She was alone and full of worry.

Not fulfilled. Not happy.

Not since his father had died.

Not since he'd pushed Graham out of the way, had been hit by the sharp barb of black magic that had been meant for his son.

And Graham hadn't been able to do the single thing his father had asked of him.

Some protector, huh?

A blip in his mind, Suz's consciousness stroking his. *"Are you okay?"*

He quickly shored up the walls around that old pain, dulling it, making sure she didn't and couldn't feel those razor-sharp memories. *"I'm fine, Firefly. Just thinking about Francis."*

A lie, and the only one she'd believe, which made him feel

like an even bigger asshole. Because now he was lying to his bondmate.

Some catch he was.

The cup *clinking* down in front of him had him blinking and refocusing. *"I'm at my mom's,"* he sent. *"I'll see you later."*

"You'd better." Her mind was light. *"I'm getting hungry."* Then she slipped away, leaving him to this conversation he didn't want to have, and yet he knew he had to face this.

Another clink, another cup, and finally, his mom sat down next to him.

And Graham didn't know how to start.

He just sat there, staring at the cup of tea he wasn't going to even pretend to drink and wondered how to broach this gulf.

"You don't even like tea, do you?" she said softly.

His head shot toward her. "What?"

"After all these years"—her gaze flicked to his cup, still full —"I didn't even know that you didn't like tea."

"I—" He fought his first instinct, which was to say, of course he liked tea then to pick up the cup and down it, just for good measure.

Her eyes went sad then closed. "Ah."

The cup was in his hand, lifting toward his mouth when she spoke again.

"Put the tea down." Graham froze at the tone of her voice, sharp and firm and—her eyes flashed open. "I mean it, honey. Put that fucking cup of tea down onto its saucer right now."

The curse had him obliging.

She didn't curse, let alone use the word fuck.

"Mom?" he asked, carefully putting it down.

A sigh. Then she covered his hand with hers and said, "I've been going to therapy."

Graham opened and closed his mouth, trying to find something to say when the announcement she'd just made had pretty much been the absolute last thing he ever would have expected.

Ever.

He'd suggested she talk to someone over the years, but that had only resulted in tears and recriminations and him immediately backing off the suggestion.

"I know it's long overdue," she said. Or rather, whispered in the direction of her hands. "But"—her eyes came up and in them was a determination he'd never seen—"I can't keep living like this."

"Um."

Not the most articulate statement at such a huge revelation, but truthfully, he was shocked. His mom had lived so long in that pattern, seemingly content, or if not that, then simply confined in her ways.

It had been nearly a hundred years of this pattern.

Of him trying to draw her out, only for her to dig in further.

To think that she could simply decide to change one day was . . . unfathomable.

"You probably think it's ridiculous that I've waited this long—"

He shook himself out of his thoughts, realized that his own life had changed in a day, hell in an *instant*. So, why couldn't someone else's? Covering her hand with his, he told her, "I think that's great, Mom."

Her throat worked on a swallow and then her gaze came up to his. "I'm sorry."

His brows drew together. "For what?"

She sighed, turned her hand over in his, squeezing his fingers lightly. "For not being the mother I should have been to you. When your father died—" Her lids closed, shoulders shuddering on an exhale. "*No.* That's not entirely true. I was always weak. I've always preferred to let my life live me rather than living it, knowing however it was going to turn out would be the way it would be. I chose to let everyone take care of me." One tear trickled down her cheek.

"Mom, it's o—"

Angrily, she wiped the tear away then looked at him again. "No, it's not okay. I wasn't a good mother to you. Not when your father was alive, not once he was gone. That's the truth, and I'm so sorry for it." She lifted her chin slightly, straightened her shoulders. "I know I can't change what I've done, but I'm going to do better for you and Amelia."

He squeezed her hand. "You were a good mom," he said, squeezing again when she snorted. "I always knew you loved us. Neither Amelia nor I ever doubted that."

"That's not enough."

"Mom," he said, wanting her to understand that he didn't blame her. It had been hard for all of them.

"Graham."

"*Mom.*"

"*Graham.*"

His lips twitched. "Is this how it's going to be?"

"I think we're both going to have to get used to the new and improved me," she said. "It turns out, I can be quite stubborn when I put my mind to it."

"Oh, that's never been in doubt."

She narrowed her eyes.

He raised his free hand, as if in surrender. "It was a compliment, I swear. Where else could I have inherited my trademark skill, if not from you?"

Slipping her hand from his, she smiled sadly and cupped his cheek. "You have so many skills, my love, so many good traits, and I'm so sorry that I didn't give you the chance to use them."

"*Mom.*"

"No, please, let me just get this out," she said, fingers trembling as she placed both of her hands on the counter. "I understand that I was lacking and wasn't nearly enough of the mother you and Amelia needed. Just as I understand that you both couldn't have possibly made it this far without resenting me. Wait," she added, when he started to protest. "I need to make sure you know that I am getting help, and I will do better, but I know that it will take time for that, just as I know that it will take you time to forgive me." She bit her lip. "Well, I hope there will come a time where you can forgive me, but—" She broke off for a moment. "But I also understand that it may not happen, and that's okay. I wasn't a parent—" Another swallow, her eyes glistening. "I couldn't be there like I should have been and—"

"I love you, Mom," he said, unable to continue watching her struggle through the words, needing her to know that. "I never resented you. It was my fa—"

But the rest of it wouldn't come.

He couldn't make this conversation about him and his feelings, absolving him of his guilt, not when his mom had just done something incredible with her life. This was about her and the giant leap forward she'd just made.

"Okay," he said, forcing lightness into his tone, "maybe I *did* resent the obsessive cleanliness extending to my room when I was a young buck, but I do think my future life partner will appreciate the cleaning skills you imparted on me."

She shuddered. "I don't think you could call that hovel your room. The *mess*."

"I know, it was terrible that I didn't have my shoes in order and had dirty laundry on the floor." He grinned.

"It was far worse than that," she said with a glare. "But I am getting help with the OCD. Suz set me up with a human therapist a few months ago, and I've been having video visits."

Surprise had his jaw dropping open. "Suz helped you with the therapist?"

His mom smiled. "Suz helps everyone." Her head tilted to the side. "But you know that already, don't you?" Eyes sparkling, she picked up his teacup and set it in the sink, but not rinsing and cleaning and then wiping the sink out like she would have done before. "The truth is that I heard Amelia talking about me with one of her friends a few months ago, after a particularly hard day. She was saying that she couldn't spend time with them because it was our night together and if she broke the schedule, I wouldn't be able to function." His mom was quiet for a moment. "I should have recognized it before, should have known what I was doing to you both."

"Maybe you weren't ready."

"Yes." A slow sigh. "I wasn't, I suppose. But that day I was— or at least fate was. Suz dropped by to return Amelia's jacket and she noticed . . . well, I don't know what she noticed exactly. All I do know is that she got me talking and then the next day she returned with Tyler, and—"

"What?" Graham asked.

"He healed me," his mom said. "He found something in my mind, an imbalance, and he fixed it, and I suddenly felt like I was able to see for the first time in my life. Everything that seemed so insurmountable, so stifling was just a little . . . *less*." She shrugged. "Then Suz gave me the name of the therapist. No, actually she scheduled the first appointment and even came to make sure I got on the call. But the rest is history. I'm working on getting better because of her."

Because of Suz.

God, his love for her grew by the second.

She'd never once said anything to him about this, never made a single mention, and she wouldn't. *Of course*, she wouldn't. Suz wouldn't even think that what she'd done for his mom was anything out of the ordinary. He'd heard her say often enough that she'd just been doing her job whenever something like this came up—whether it was planning Francis's funeral or arranging for Felicia and Hank to have meals delivered so they could bond with their newborn.

But this . . . doing *this* for his family, for him, and he was undone.

"I had no idea, Mom," he said with a blip of guilt. "I'm sorry I didn't notice your progress, didn't support you—"

"Oh honey, that's not what this is about. Don't take another thing on your shoulders." She pushed back a strand of her hair. "I hid what I was doing because I was worried I would mess it up, that I would fail you and Amelia again and—" She shook her head. "Anyway, I'm telling you now because I'm finally ready and happy enough with my progress."

"I understand," he said. "And I'm glad you're ready to share it with me."

Her shoulders lifted and fell on an exhale. "Of course, I still have the OCD and anxiety—both of which will probably never go away completely, but between the healing and the therapy, I'm . . . I don't know . . . I'm different. Me, but more."

Standing, Graham circled the counter and pulled her into a hug. "I'm so proud of you," he told her. "I can't begin to imagine how hard it must have been to get better."

"I'm not there yet."

He leaned back, glanced into her eyes. "There?"

"Not better yet," she said. "But I will be."

And for the first time in his life, he knew she would.

"Now," she said, releasing him and stepping back. She turned for the fridge and opened it, reaching into the way back. "I'm not the only one with an eventful life of late." She straightened with a beer in hand, passing it over to him. "That was supposed to be for my pasta sauce, but I think you'd prefer it over tea, yeah?"

"Yeah." He grinned and popped the top, lifting it to his lips.

Then nearly choking to death when she asked, "When were you going to tell me about the bond?"

After his mom stopped laughing, and after he'd wiped the beer dripping out his nose, they both sat down again, plowed through that plate of cookies, and he told his mom about how the bond came to be.

The G-rated version, anyway.

NINETEEN

Suz

SHE REACHED OVER and patted Dee's hand. "How are you doing?"

Suz, Gabby, Alex, and Daughtry were gathered for their weekly reality TV binge. It was Suz's turn to host the gathering, and they were meeting to consume the season finale of their favorite, *Librarians Gone Wild*. The show was delivering its usual mix of horror (torn pages and dog-eared corners), hilarity (who was caught trying to smuggle *what* into the bathroom?), and all the feels (that long-missing copy of *Pride and Prejudice* finally found its way back into the drop box).

But while they had their normal mix of junk food and entertainment, none of them were feeling particularly festive.

Dee sighed, her violet eyes sad. She had worked closely with Francis, same as all of them, but her bond with the trainer went perhaps deeper than anyone else in their friend group. "I'm okay," she whispered. "I just still can't believe he's gone."

Gabby nodded sadly. "I'm going to miss him."

Suz was, too. They all were.

"How are the kids?" Alex asked.

Dee nodded. "Doing better than the adults, I think. This has been a tough year with the evacuations and the attack and now Francis, but they're hanging in there. I still can't believe that Dante has asked me to take over for him. I didn't even know I wasn't human until . . . what . . . a year ago?" She shook her head. "And I've spent most of that year fumbling around with my powers."

Dee was the most powerful Rengalla in the Colony.

She had the gift of foresight. On the scale of magic— primary for the elements, secondary for skills like healing and teleportation, tertiary for oracles—Daughtry was the only Rengalla on the planet alive with that ability.

But that power came with a cost.

One that had nearly destroyed her until she'd navigated her way through it.

Now she was stable, bonded, happy, and her ability for foresight was safely walled away.

Because sometimes, knowing the future was the worst kind of torture.

"You've gained control," Alex, who was also Daughtry's sister, said. "That's not easy for a normal Rengalla, let alone for someone with your skills."

Suz nodded. "I agree. I think you're the perfect person to take his place. You know the struggle for control. You've mastered the primary skills and have some capacity for the secondary."

"But not all."

"That's true," Suz agreed. "But no one has all those skills. Which is why the different specialties each have their own lead, right?"

A sigh. "That's true." Dee sighed again. "I just . . . I just don't want him to be gone."

Suz's eyes prickled, same as they had each time someone said the same.

The guilt hadn't eased, and she knew from her experience in treating humans in the outside world that it wouldn't for a long time. She'd dream of every action, of every possibility until, ultimately, she exhausted all the angles and was able to breathe again, to sleep soundly and wake up refreshed. Eventually, she would begin to feel like herself again.

But eventually was a long way away.

And it had been ages since she'd had to deal with losing someone.

Certainly, there had been touch and go situations in the past, but she hadn't lost a Rengalla since she'd ascended the role of senior healer, hadn't felt the burden on her shoulders.

The losses had been on Doreen's.

Dee's eyes drifted to Suz's and though she tried to look away, it wasn't in time for her friend not to see that pain.

"Shit, I'm sorry," Dee said, throwing an arm around her shoulders.

"It's not—" But to Suz's horror, her voice broke.

The room went even quieter when Gabby turned off the show.

"*I'm* the one who's sorry," Suz whispered. "I should have—" More horror as a tear slipped down her cheek. "I—"

Graham's voice flared to life in her mind. "*Firefly?*"

"*I'm fine.*"

But she wasn't fine. She was crying in earnest now and hating herself for it. She'd gotten through the first two weeks, was nearly through the third one. She just needed to hold on and stay strong, and this would all get better.

Dee hugged her tightly. Gabby handed her a tissue. Alex patted her awkwardly on the knee.

She recognized each of the gestures, tried to slow her

breathing, to halt her tears. The last thing she wanted to do was to cause them further distress. They were hurting, and she should be the strong one.

But the tears wouldn't stop.

"It's okay," Dee was whispering.

"Just let it out," Gabby said. "You'll feel better and—"

The door to her room flew open, crashing into the wall with a *thud* that had her eyes flying open. Alex was on her feet, protecting them like the soldier she was, but she immediately relaxed when she saw that it was Graham in the hall.

His expression was fierce, golden eyes darkened and molten, his exposed skin was covered in a coating of sweat that made it gilt and smooth like a gorgeous statue and his shirt stuck to his body, highlighting every taut muscle. But all of that outer beauty was nothing compared to what she felt in her mind.

Peace.

He was sending her peace and comfort and taking away the pain.

She didn't understand *how* he was doing it, how he could be healing her from the inside out, how he could be taking her emotional pain when he hadn't ever shown an inclination for healing before.

Sometimes mates were able to use their partner's powers for short periods to pick up an additional skill.

But this was different.

She couldn't heal the heart.

And it felt as though he were determinedly piecing hers back together.

Then his arms were around her, and he was stitching his soul to hers, tying them together.

Forever.

Her breath caught when his mind surged into hers. Not the trickle, the ebb and flow of him she had been getting for the last two weeks. This was Graham, every single part of him, and his consciousness was wrapping hers tight, holding her close, and she had never *ever* felt safer.

"You've been holding it together," he whispered, and she opened her eyes, saw the room was empty. Her friends must have beat a hasty retreat at the sight of him in all his sweaty, golden gloriousness.

She pushed against his chest, but he didn't let her go. Instead, he handed her a box of tissues and she dabbed her eyes.

Okay, fine, she blotted her eyes and wiped the very unattractive trail of snot from her nose.

Pretty crier, she was not.

"I'm really done with the tears lately."

"I don't mind."

She sighed and pushed his chest again.

He didn't let her go.

Again.

"You don't have to be strong all the time."

"Well, I'd like to be strong *some* of the time with you," she grumbled. "I'm tired of playing the watering pot."

"What you are is *tired*," he said. "You haven't been sleeping well."

"You haven't been there," she said, still grumbling. "You slept with me that first day after Francis then you had to go and be all *thoughtful* by sleeping in your own rooms. *I know you're used to your own space, Suz,*" she said, mimicking his voice. *"This is all new, so I'll give you time before I torture you with my presence."* Her nose wrinkled. "But no, you had to hook me on the scent and feel of you that first day. Now, my bed feels empty! So, any lack of sleep is your fault."

He kissed the top of your head. "Nice try."

"It's not a try." She snuggled closer. "I like having you there. I know these last few weeks have been challenging for everyone, but I would like to spend more time with you moving forward." She bit her lip, figured what the hell and said what was in her mind and heart, "I miss you when you're not there."

"Well, I do think you liked me holding you and eating the food I bring you, despite the larger jeans in your future," he said lightly. "But the rest of it is nonsense. Or at least, *my* part of it is."

She frowned. "What are you talking about?"

"I just left my mom's," he said. "Well really, I ran out of her rooms when I felt you hurting, but that's not the point I'm trying to get at."

"What *is* the point?"

He sighed, his mind going carefully blank. "The point is that I haven't really been trying to give you space and time. I've been purposefully keeping my distance," he said. "I needed to in order to keep my sanity."

For a moment, she didn't process his words. Then she did, and a wave of embarrassment covered her from head to toe.

Keeping his distance in order to hold on to his *sanity*?

Sweet Christ, was it that bad being bonded with her?

She shoved out of his arms, the bolt of pain shooting straight through her before disappointment took its place, filling her until it felt like her skin would burst. She'd known. She'd known it was too good to be true, knew it was impossible for someone—

Fuck that.

She *was* loveable.

Graham's voice was very close to her ear. "That's not what I mean, Firefly."

"You should go." Her voice was steady. "I'm fine now. Thanks for the . . . assistance."

Graham cursed and grabbed her arm. "Fuck, Suz, I'm trying to tell you—"

She moved toward the door.

"Just stop for a second," he said. "This isn't about you, it's about me, okay?"

She huffed out an annoyed breath, glared at him. "*That's what you're going with? It's not you, it's me?*" She crossed her arms. "*Seriously?*"

"That's not—" He broke off, cursed again.

"No need to spare my feelings," she said. "We'll find a way to make the bond *palatable* for us both in order to keep our magic."

One hand clamped down on her shoulder as she wrenched open the door. His other slammed it shut, and then his chest was pinning the front of her body to the wooden panel, his hot breath in her ear, one palm shifting to her hip, the other pressed flat by her head. "I don't want fucking palatable, Suz. I want you, and I'm trying to tell you how much, even though clearly I'm doing it in a fucked-up way."

She struggled against him. "To keep your *sanity?*" she spat.

"Yes."

Was it possible for this man to hurt her even more? She'd given everything she knew how to give, and still it wasn't enough.

"Stop," he growled. "Stop thinking of yourself like that. You are the most amazing woman I've ever met. You are smart and kind and strong and—"

"Driving you insane!" she shouted, pushing him off her with some sort of herculean burst of strength. She poked him in the chest. "What kind of mate drives their other half insane? So clearly, there's something wrong with me! Don't even try to deny it—"

"There is absolutely nothing wrong with you!" he roared. "The problem is with me, with my fucking inability to keep the people I love safe, to make sure those I'm supposed to be protecting are happy and well and—" He broke off with a curse, turning away and shoving a hand through his hair. "I'm filled with guilt because I made two vows in my life, and I broke both of those. And because of it . . ."

Her heart was pounding.

Pain was radiating through her in waves, but it wasn't her pain this time. Instead, it was coming from Graham, and wave after wave was barraging her, stealing her breath and nearly taking her to her knees.

"Because of what?" she asked when he just stood there like a statue.

He didn't move. "I failed both of my parents."

Six words so flatly spoken and yet not telling her anything, or at least not filling in any of the details that could explain why he was hurting so deeply.

"How?" she asked, closing the distance between them and placing a gentle hand on his back.

"In different ways," he whispered, still not looking at her and not adding anything to the statement for so long that she thought for a moment he wouldn't say anything further. But then he said, "My father died because of me, and my mother lived half a life because of it."

Oh.

Oh.

Also, fuck.

She slipped around to his front, snagging his hand and tugging him toward the bed. "How did your father die?"

He allowed her to sit him on the mattress and wound an arm around her, tugging her into his lap when she would have sat next to him. "In the war," he said, and she immediately knew which war, which battle. She'd been a child, but their people had suffered a great many losses. And Graham's father had been one of them.

"I'm sorry."

"I'm not the only one. The triplets lost their dad, many others lost people important to them."

"But that doesn't mean it's easy."

"No, it doesn't," he agreed. "I was there, too," he said. "I fought alongside him, was supposed to have his back."

Her throat went dry, her pulse pounding, because she knew this was about to get a lot worse. "What happened, honey?"

"The battle was over, or so I thought. We'd rounded up the Dalshie, freed the prisoners, were getting ready to leave. And . . . I let my guard down." His fingers clenched on her hips, and she got a glimpse of the memory in his mind. It drifted across their connection like a dark smoke, filled with pain and noise and fear and . . . despair. "I didn't see the bolt of magic until it was too late. But my dad did, and he pushed me out of the way."

"Oh, Graham," she whispered.

"I vowed to my mom to bring him home safe. And I failed." A muscle in his jaw throbbed. "The magic nearly sliced him in two, but he suffered, death didn't take him right away."

Her throat burned. "Baby, I'm so sorry."

"It was horrible," he said, succinctly, that muscle still pulsing, "but the worst part was that he asked me to look after my mom and sister, to keep them safe."

She brushed a finger over that twitching muscle. "And you did a great job of it."

"No!" he burst out. "No." Softer now, his mind rubbing against hers in equal parts misery and apology. "But don't you see? I didn't keep my mom safe, didn't help her live a happy life. She was a prisoner in her own mind, of her own fears for *years*."

"Your mom . . ." She bit her lip, wanting to reassure him but also not wanting to share private information he may not be privy to.

He cupped her cheek. "She told me, Firefly. Told me all you did for her."

"I just made a phone call."

"No," he said. "You did so much more than that."

A shake of her head. "I did my job. That's it."

She felt his smile in her mind. "I knew you'd say that."

"Graham . . . I don't understand."

He touched her cheek. "I tried for years to have her talk to someone, and you had one conversation with her and changed her mind. I might be jealous if I weren't so grateful. I've never seen her happier, never seen her able to leave her rooms without that crippling anxiety. She's getting better."

"Tyler did that."

"And you," he said. "You set up the appointments."

"All I did—"

"No, *all* you did was change someone's life. Don't minimize it. I'm in absolute awe of you, sweetheart. I see you helping people, not ever expecting anything in return, and never stopping." He pressed a kiss to her forehead. "But you're more than just a healer. You're a good person, a good friend, and I feel so fucking lucky to be bonded with you."

"Graham," she whispered. "Don't you see that I feel the same? Hardly anyone has ever seen me as more than the job, certainly not the men in my life. But you understand that I can't separate the two, and you don't hold it against me when I work late."

He shrugged. "I'll just come and pester you until I convince you to leave."

"See?" She smiled. "Plus, you force feed me food and make sure I get enough sleep, not to mention making me laugh and hauling me outside to get some sunshine on this pasty skin. But it's more than that. I've always been the one to take care of everyone else, to give. To know that you're giving too makes all the difference. Makes it okay that"—she tapped her forehead —"you're in here"—her heart—"and here. And that makes me not terrified of that closeness for once in my life. You give me the strength to give you everything."

"But don't you see?" he asked, the words agonized, his mind twisted up.

"See what?"

"See that I'm nowhere near worthy enough for you."

She froze. "Why?"

Silence.

"Because I couldn't keep them safe."

"That wasn't your fault."

"Because I couldn't give you what you needed."

She frowned.

"You needed me to let you in, but I walled you out," he blurted, the words coming in rapid succession. "You needed to know that I appreciated you, but I let you think you weren't good enough for me. You needed me in your bed, but I avoided the contact, worried you'd see the truth."

"The truth being that *you* weren't good enough for *me*."

"Yes!" He shifted, dumping her to the mattress and standing up. "Yes, I'm not good enough. Yes, you should be with someone better. Yes, I can't keep you safe, and if you get hurt or sick, then I will have failed again and—"

"You're scared."

"Yes!" he blurted again, skidding to a stop, his gaze on his hands.

"Well, that makes two of us," she said, pushing to her feet and crossing over to him. "But that's a good thing."

Those golden eyes shot to hers.

"Because there are two of us in this relationship, and that means it will take two of us to make it work." Suz moved closer, resting her hands on his biceps. "Two of us to share those fears and painful memories, two of us to care for each other, two of us to find our way to happy." Her lips curved. "Two of us to screw up."

His mind throbbed against hers, absorbing her words, feeling the certainty in her mind of her statements. "You make it sound easy."

She laughed. "I'm sure it will be fucking brutal."

He grinned. "You mean the tendency for us to both pretend we're doing totally fine."

"Yup." A nod. "We're fine until all of our emotions are bottled up so fiercely, they blow the cork and burst everywhere."

"I'm not sure that's the proper analogy," he said, his arms coming around her, tugging her close.

She smiled, moved a little closer. "No, it's probably not."

"You know, Francis isn't your fault," he whispered, tucking a strand of hair behind her ear.

"I'm working on accepting that." A beat, her gaze holding his. "Just like you know the same is true of your parents."

His breath caught, his mind thudding against hers, even as his mouth tipped up. "Seems like there are two of us in this room working on accepting truths."

"I love you," she whispered.

His lips parted, a breath escaping. Then he grinned and pulled her even closer. "I *fucking* love you," he said and kissed her, their lips and tongues tangling, his hands holding her close. He kissed her until her lungs screamed for air, kissed her long after she decided she didn't need oxygen anyway. And when he finally released her, he did it slowly, their lips clinging together, their minds intertwined, his fingers in her hair, their bodies flush together. "I love you even if you ruined the plans I'd made of confessing that to you under a moonlit sky with chocolates and a bottle of champagne."

"I would never turn down chocolate and champagne," she said, after her pulse had settled and she could breathe well enough to speak. "But can we agree to not hold tight to plans and expectations and instead to just live our lives? Together," she added in case he was going to be stubborn about it.

But this was Graham. Easy-going, liked by everyone Graham. He didn't do stubborn—or not *too* often anyway.

Instead, he said, "Together sounds perfect."

Then he kissed her again, kissed her until they fell into bed together, until they were both naked and filled to the brim with desire. Kissed her until their bodies came together, until that desire exploded and consumed them both with pleasure.

And afterward, he wrapped her in his arms and stayed.

Her eyes slid closed, and she nuzzled against his neck. *"And just so you know, your dad would be so proud of the man you've become."*

His mind flared, but he didn't argue with her.

Instead, he held her closer. *"I love you, Firefly."*

"Someday I'll get the truth of that name out of you."

A laugh, out loud and along their bond. *"Maybe."*

Then they both fell asleep, and when she woke, still in his arms, she felt absolutely rested.

TWENTY

Graham

SHE SPUN AROUND, a huge grin on her face, her hands plunking onto her hips.

Graham stopped in the hallway of the infirmary, a bundle in his hands. "How'd you know I was here?"

She shot him a look, tapped her temple. "There's no sneaking up on me now."

He smirked. "I'll find a way."

Suz rolled her eyes but walked down the hallway and wrapped her arms around him, kissing him soundly on the lips. "Hi," she whispered after she'd pulled back, ignoring the catcalls coming from the waiting room. "I missed you."

They'd had their talk nearly two weeks before, and things had only gotten better since then.

No more secrets.

No more holding himself back.

Just him and this woman and their connection growing stronger every day.

"Hi," he whispered back, taking her arm and leading her toward her office.

"No hanky panky!" someone called. "My appointment is in ten minutes."

Grinning, he waved at the room over his shoulder, not bothering to look back. "We won't be but a minute."

"Likely story," the voice muttered.

Suz laughed, said quietly, "If only they knew the kind of hanky panky that started this mess."

"Should we give them something to talk about?" he asked, tugging her into the office and shutting the door. He closed the distance between them, let his mouth linger a hairsbreadth from hers.

"Stop it, you." But she was grinning, and her mind was light.

"I have something for you," they said at the same time.

Then froze, grins breaking out on their faces.

"I get to go first," Suz said, shifting out of his hold and moving to her desk. "Since you're always bringing me things."

"So bossy."

"Shush," she said, opening a drawer and indicating he should sit. "Now, close your eyes."

He knew her well enough by now to not bother arguing. He shut his eyes.

"Hold out your hands."

He held out his hands.

She placed something in them.

"Okay, open."

He opened. And . . . emotions tore through him. She'd given him a photograph, neatly framed in pale gray, a thin piece of glass protecting the image inside, but he knew he was focusing on the unimportant details because it was the image itself that had struck him mute.

"Your mom found it," she said quietly. "She wanted you to have it. I just had it restored and framed."

His lungs were frozen, and it took him a moment to remember how to breathe. "This was taken the first day I made soldier," he whispered. "My dad was so proud of me."

"I can see that in his smile."

Graham could, too. Their arms were around each other, their postures relaxed, huge smiles on their faces. He jumped to his feet, hugged her tight. "Thank you, Firefly."

"I love you."

He ran his fingers over her jaw. "You know *you're welcome* is a more customary response."

"I prefer *I love you*."

He waggled brows. "Me, too."

She laughed in his mind, even though in front of him, she just shook her head. "You're terrible."

"No," he said, "what I am is touched and also certain that my gift isn't nearly so nice."

"I don't need anything—"

There was a knock at the door, Gabby's voice pitched loud enough they could hear it through the panel. "Bernadette is getting restless."

He released her, thrust the package he'd brought into her hands. "We've got to get on with it before the troops storm the castle."

"Hmm," she murmured. "You'd fight them off."

"Even I am not stupid enough to take on Bernadette."

She giggled but got on with opening the package, and he felt in his heart and mind the moment she saw what was inside.

"Oh, Graham," she whispered, pulling out the thin metal ring he'd had made for her. Made of delicate silver with diamonds forming the wings, he'd also had a gem that exactly matched her eyes set in the firefly's belly.

"Can I?" he asked.

Her fingers trembled when she extended them. "I know that Rengalla don't often have weddings," he whispered, sliding it down her ring finger, "though I'm game, if you are."

She shook her head. "*God*, no. Amelia is already going insane planning a bonding ceremony. I don't want a wedding in her grasp."

Amusement curled through him, intertwined with his love for her. "That's what I figured. So, this is to remind you of me."

Suz laughed. "As if I could ever forget you."

"Okay, so it's to tell all the other men you're mine."

One brown brow lifted. "Since the bond magic of a billboard has faded."

"Exactly." He touched the band. "I think the manly side of the bondmate relationship is allowed to be possessive."

"And so is the female side," she said, winding her arms around him.

"Guess you'd better get me a ring then."

Her mouth twitched. "I guess so."

"I love you," he murmured, brushing his lips across hers.

"I know you do," she said, eyes dancing with mischief. "Which means that you're going to tell me right now what Firefly means."

"I am?"

"Yup."

He shrugged. "Okay, it means—"

A knock thudded. "It's been eleven minutes!" came Bernadette's voice.

"You've got to be kidding me," she muttered, then louder. "Just a minute," she called.

"I'll give you exactly one, then I'm busting down the door."

He raised a brow. "Saved by the Bernadette?"

"Saved by the Bernadette," she murmured, and with a

rueful smile, Suz brushed one more kiss across his mouth and then pulled away. "Duty calls."

"I'll see you tonight, Firefly."

A scowl. A kiss across the bond.

And then she was back to her patients.

And he saw himself out.

As one did when they were bonded with the Rengalla's senior healer.

TWENTY-ONE

Suz

LIFE WAS BETTER than she could have ever imagined.

It had been a month since Graham had surprised her with the firefly ring, and they'd settled into a routine that had gotten better as each day passed.

He'd moved into her rooms, since they were closer to the infirmary, and he'd accepted Dante's offer to become the newest LexTal. Something that was long overdue in her opinion, but she was just glad that Graham was living his life, well, living *their* life.

Because they were intertwined.

Because their bond had grown and strengthened.

She could feel him even now, and she was a fair distance from the Colony, in the furthest quadrant, hiking her way through an easy trail.

Easy because she was out of practice.

Hiking because she'd hired help, and she actually had a day off.

And the sun felt glorious on her face, the gentle breeze refreshing as she broke into a slight sweat from her exertion. Which clearly meant that she needed to do this more often if this easy-ass hike was getting her tired.

She could be on her feet all day in the infirmary, but give her a tiny hill and—

"How are you doing, Firefly?"

Grinning at the sound of Graham's voice, she paused to take a breath and decided to have a sit down on the plush stretch of greenery to the side of the trail. That tree would make the perfect backrest for her to watch the clouds float by.

"I'm good, honey," she thought, dropping her pack and sitting down. Her ring flashed in the sunlight and she sighed, knowing her smile had turned "dopey."

Gabby's words, not hers.

But since her friend had a similar dopey smile on her face when she was talking to her mate, Suz couldn't complain.

Too much.

"Don't hike too long," he thought. *"You need to have energy for tonight."*

"Oh?"

"Yes. Oh."

She snorted. *"Okay, I'll pace myself."*

"Good of you to listen and obey." He merely chuckled at her mental swat then kept thinking. *"But seriously, enjoy your day. Telepath if you need me."*

"I will—" She froze.

"What is it?" His mental voice had gone from teasing to serious in a heartbeat.

"I thought I heard some—"

Crack.

Her breath froze.

"Suz."

She shot to her feet. *"There's something out here."*

"Head back into the Colony. Right now."

The rustling, the heavy thumps continued. Something big was coming her way, and fast. She left her pack and stepped back onto the trail, turning back toward civilization and hauling ass back the direction she'd walked.

"Suz?"

"I'm on the trail, moving away from the noise." She thought the noise might actually still be getting closer. *"I left my pack. I should have—"*

"No, you need to move with speed," Graham told her. *"Morgan is on perimeter. I'm sending him your way."*

"It's probably nothing—"

But she didn't get to finish the thought because the noise made its appearance with a roar.

Terror gripped her in its claws when she looked back to see a huge black bear had burst onto the trail.

And it was thundering toward her.

"It's a bear!"

"I'm coming. I'll be there."

She stopped running, turned to face it while slowly backing up. The shield was supposed to keep these big animals out—and let the small ones come and go as they pleased—but every once in a while, a cub got trapped inside the shield and grew too large to leave, requiring it to make its home inside for a short while.

The soldiers did regular sweeps for the critters, but somehow this one must have outsmarted them all.

And it was closing in on her.

She threw her hands up, yelled. "Hey, bear! Stay back!"

It slowed, no longer sprinting for her but not turning around and leaving her alone.

Curious.

But even a little bit of curious from a large bear could bring big trouble.

"It'll be okay, baby. I'm coming." Graham's voice was calm, but she could feel his panic, knew that this was his worst nightmare, not being able to protect her and—

The bear charged.

She screamed, released a burst of air magic, knocking it back several yards. It rose to its feet, shook itself, and . . .

Continued following her.

And heart in her throat, she continued backing up, moving down the hill, wishing her hike had been closer because she was still too fucking far away.

One eye on the bear. One on the trail. One, when she could spare it, searching for a weapon that could help her. One on her magic in her mind, trying to figure out what she could do to protect herself.

The bear charged again.

And . . . she felt it.

Graham's magic.

Graham's *earth* magic.

She gripped it tight, and with the bear closing in, she let her instincts drive her actions.

Gold and brown magic shot from her palms, pushing the bear back several meters again. In the space she'd gained, her powers expanded to the sides of the trail, yanking on trees and vines, tearing them from the earth and bringing them forward. They flew toward the bear, the vines catching its feet, knocking it to the ground. The trees followed, stacking together, building a heavy wooden cage around the bear.

Like Lincoln Logs.

Only with huge trees and vines and dirt holding them in place.

The magic cut off.

Her knees buckled, head swimming from the massive surge of magic.

The bear roared.

And she lost consciousness.

TWENTY-TWO

Graham

HE SKIDDED to a stop on the trail less than five minutes after Morgan had called to say that Suz was all right.

But he didn't actually breathe easy until he saw her, rubbing her temples and sitting up.

Falling to his knees beside her, he scooped her off Morgan's lap with a glare at the other man—unnecessary, he knew, but the man had his hands on his woman—and gently probed her mind at the same time he spoke out loud. "Are you okay?"

He could barely feel her on the bond, her side of the connection weak and thready.

"I used too much magic," she groaned, rubbing her forehead. "Then I decided I'd like to take a tumble to this hard ass ground."

Nodding, he took stock of her body, searching for any injuries, but aside from a cut on her cheek and scraped palms, she didn't appear to be any worse for wear. She certainly hadn't been clawed open, as he'd been picturing the entire run over here.

"I'm sorry I wasn't here," he said, knowing he was still frantically running his hands over her, still probing at her mind. But even though he didn't find any additional injuries, even though he could feel the magic pouring back into her, replenishing her reserves, he couldn't stop himself from touching her.

Failed.

Failure.

"I should have been here," he said, not caring that Morgan was there, that he'd hear. Their connection was still weak, and he needed to say this, even if it was aloud. "I'm supposed to protect you and—"

She pressed her finger to his lips. "Don't you see?" she asked. "You protected me."

He frowned, knowing she was concussed. "No, that was Morgan. He got here—"

"No," she said, pushing up. "That was *you*. Your magic protected me. Your magic helped me make"—she waved a hand at the pile of logs—"*that*. If you weren't in my mind, if I didn't have your powers laced with mine . . . I wouldn't have gotten away."

"*You* made that?" he asked.

"*We* made it," she said, starting to stand, albeit on shaky legs. Not that it mattered, he'd hold her up. He'd be her shield.

The bear roared from inside its prison.

Suz jumped, wavered on her feet.

The hell with it, he swept her up into his arms.

She didn't complain, just rested her head on his shoulder. "I'm taking her back to the Colony," he called.

Morgan lifted his cell. "Dante is almost here anyway."

Nodding, he carried Suz down the trail, passing Dante and Cody a few minutes later. Dante had a tranquilizer gun in his hands, and Graham knew that would knock the bear out and then Cody would open the shield enough to get it on the proper side.

Not that he cared.

"You're never hiking without me again," he snapped.

Suz simply said, "Of course, I am."

He stopped, started to argue, then decided he needed to have her safe while he argued with her. "Suz."

"Graham."

He scowled.

"I'll allow you to go a little crazy for a few more minutes, since that was scary and you're a big protective man," she said. "But only for a *few* more minutes because you, more than anyone, know that I can't live my life by hiding away."

"But—"

She placed her hand over his chest. "Even when you weren't physically there, you were in my mind," she said. "You protected me. You *saved* me."

His pulse began to slow. "I love you, Firefly," he whispered.

"I know."

He slowed his pace from jog to walk, and after a few minutes, he let Suz make her own way, or at least let her traverse the trail on her own two feet with his arm around her waist. Eventually, his panic began to ebb, albeit at a marginal rate.

"See?" Suz asked. "It wasn't so bad."

Graham thought of the terror he'd experienced over the last half hour. "Oh, it was *so bad*, worse than *so bad*, my love."

"I know." A beat. "I was pretty scared myself."

He held her a little closer. "I'm proud of you."

She laughed. "Apparently, I can take on bears and survive to laugh about it." A glance up at him. "So, you'd better watch out next time you cross me."

"I wouldn't dare cross you."

"Good answer."

They kept walking and pretty soon, they were nearing the front entrance of the Colony, and he decided that he might as well tell her. There would never be—better never be—a more perfect moment to do so.

He tugged her to a stop.

Chocolate brown eyes found his.

"I call you Firefly because you seem normal on the surface, a beautiful woman for certain, there is never any doubt of that. But your true beauty comes in the darkness, in tough times, when others feel as though they're ready to give in." He cupped her cheek. "That's when the light in you burns brightest. That's when you lead everyone around you out of the shadows."

"Graham," she whispered, tears leaking out the corners of those stunning brown eyes.

"I love you," he said, "and I will love you until the day they put me in the ground."

She sniffed, threw her arms around him, her tears soaking into his shirt. "So long as it's not because of a bear."

He laughed, so much joy in his heart.

And then he *felt*, with so much affection in that heart, when she added, "I am *so* in love with you, Crumbles."

"Forever and always," he said.

"Forever and always."

TO SMOKE

Darcy

SHE SET the pan down that she was scrubbing and rested her chin on her chest, her arms aching.

It was her turn in the kitchens.

As an intermediate soldier, she only spent part of her time on patrols and protecting her people. The rest of the time was passed here in the kitchen, under Lex's tutelage. She didn't mind—the orders or the pot scrubbing. Cooking reminded her of her mom, and she missed her, and the orders . . . well, they reminded her of her mom as well.

There was a reason she was a good soldier.

Ha.

Not so much.

She knew she had a chip on her shoulder a mile wide, knew she questioned the orders given her far too often—though she *had* gotten better at the timing of said questions. There was a reason her peers had achieved senior soldier status while she hadn't as of yet.

But in the grand scheme of things, she wasn't in any hurry.

She preferred things on her own timeframe, and with the extended life of a Rengalla, truly, what was the hurry?

Or at least, that was what she told herself.

Because the truth was that she was getting a bit . . . tetchy.

The knock of the counter made her jump, her hands splashing water from the basin and soaking her front.

She narrowed her eyes, glared at the intruder.

Not that it would matter.

Morgan never cared that he'd annoyed her.

Nope. The man lived to press her buttons, to infuriate. Ever since—

And she wasn't going to cross that particular mental minefield. No freaking way.

"Earth to Darcy," he said. "Mooning over the latest boy band? Dreaming of whether your last name will be Carter or Timberlake, or maybe you've gone modern and it will be Styles."

"Ugh," she muttered, picking up the next pot. "What do you want?"

He shrugged. "To torment you."

"Well, luckily, I'm familiar enough with that course of action."

He laughed, and the sound slid down her spine like honey. The man had always been too gorgeous for words and too dangerous for her self-control.

"What do you want?"

Another shrug and he picked up the pot she'd scrubbed already and left to dry on the rack and began wiping it down. Then he did the next one, as she continued washing.

Scrub. Rinse. Dry. Put away.

Until her job was done.

And still, he didn't say anything.

Well, that was fine. She didn't say anything either. Just did her task, hung up her apron, and turned for the exit. If he wanted to languish his time away in the kitchens, that was fine by her.

But she was tired, and she was leaving.

Unfortunately, he followed her out into the hall.

"Morgan," she said on a sigh.

He chuckled. "If I had a penny for every time I heard that tone."

Darcy rolled her eyes but didn't bite.

Morgan continued walking by her side, weaving through the quiet corridors of the Colony. It was late, well after dinner service, and most people were back in their rooms.

But not her.

And not Morgan, who dogged her every step.

Until they finally reached her quarters.

She stopped in front of her door, plunked her hands on her hips, and glared at him. "I'm tired, and I don't have time for your bullshit."

Normally, he would have laughed again, would have made a snarky comment.

But instead, he smiled at her, his gorgeous hazel eyes soft and intense, and she felt a bolt of electricity shoot through her.

What?

She didn't get any further than that, because he ran the backs of his knuckles over her cheek. "I know you don't, Pem," he murmured, making her frown at the name. He'd never called her that before, even when—

She shook her head, opened her mouth.

He beat her to the reply. "But you should know that I'll always have time for yours."

"I—"

"This is for you."

He shoved an envelope into her hands.

"What—?"

Then he was gone, long legs eating up the hall, disappearing around the corner. Shaken, she unlocked her door, moved inside her room, and collapsed onto the bed where she opened the envelope.

And felt the bottom drop out of her world.

—To Smoke Coming October 18th 2021.

TO SMOKE

To Smoke is coming October 18th, 2021. Preorder your copy at
www.books2read.com/tosmoke

ALSO BY ELISE FABER

Charging

Caged (March 12th, 2021)

Love, Action, Camera (all stand alone)

Dotted Line

Action Shot

Close-Up

End Scene

Meet Cute (April 5th, 2021)

Love After Midnight **(all stand alone)**

Rum And Notes

Virgin Daiquiri

On The Rocks

Sex On The Seats (April 26th, 2021)

Life Sucks Series **(all stand alone)**

Train Wreck

Hot Mess

Dumpster Fire (February 15th, 2021)

Clusterf*@k (August 16th, 2021)

Roosevelt Ranch Series **(all stand alone, series complete)**

Disaster at Roosevelt Ranch

Heartbreak at Roosevelt Ranch

Collision at Roosevelt Ranch

Regret at Roosevelt Ranch

Desire at Roosevelt Ranch

Phoenix Series (read in order)

Phoenix Rising

Dark Phoenix

Phoenix Freed

Phoenix: LexTal Chronicles (rereleasing soon, stand alone, Phoenix world)

From Ashes

In Flames (January 25th, 2021)

To Smoke (October 18th, 2021)

KTS Series

Fire and Ice (Hurt Anthology, stand alone)

Riding The Edge (December 7th, 2020)

Stand Alones

Someday, Maybe (YA)

ABOUT THE AUTHOR

USA Today bestselling author, Elise Faber, loves chocolate, Star Wars, Harry Potter, and hockey (the order depending on the day and how well her team -- the Sharks! -- are playing). She and her husband also play as much hockey as they can squeeze into their schedules, so much so that their typical date night is spent on the ice. Elise changes her hair color more often than some people change their socks, loves sparkly things, and is the mom to two exuberant boys. She lives in Northern California. Connect with her in her Facebook group, the Fabinators or find more information about her books at www.elisefaber.com.

facebook.com/elisefaberauthor

amazon.com/author/elisefaber

bookbub.com/profile/elise-faber

instagram.com/elisefaber

goodreads.com/elisefaber

pinterest.com/elisefaberwrite